ZOM-B
MISSION
DARREN SHAN

SIMON AND SCHUSTER

First published in Great Britain in 2014 by Simon & Schuster UK Ltd
A CBS COMPANY

Copyright © 2014 by Darren Shan

Illustrations © Warren Pleece

1 3 5 7 9 10 8 6 4 2

Simon & Schuster UK Ltd
1st Floor
222 Gray's Inn Road
London WC1X 8HB

www.simonandschuster.co.uk

Simon & Schuster Australia, Sydney
Simon & Schuster India, New Delhi

A CIP catalogue copy for this book
is available from the British Library.

HB ISBN: 978-0-85707-776-9
TPB ISBN: 978-0-85707-777-6
EBOOK ISBN: 978-0-85707-779-0

Printed and bound by CPI Group (UK) Ltd, Croydon, CR0 4YY

For:
the real Biddy Barry, AKA Momma Shan!

OBE (Order of the Bloody Entrails) to:
Nick Stearn – a designer on a mission!

Editorial missionaries:
Venetia Gosling
Kate Sullivan
plus new zombie on the block
Elv Moody

Mission control:
the Christopher Little Agency.

THEN . . .

Becky Smith's father was a bully and a racist. She lived a double life under his reign. For instance her best friend, Vinyl, was black, so she could never talk about him at home. Her favourite teacher, Mr Burke, was of mixed race, so she had to pretend to dislike him.

B never stood up to her abusive father. It was easier to play along and act as if she was racist too. She didn't think any harm could come of it. Until the day of the zombie uprising. As she was trying to escape from her school, her dad screamed at her to throw a black boy to a pack of advancing zombies to stall them. Accustomed to doing whatever he told her, she obeyed.

Horrified by what she had done, B at last told her father what she truly thought of him and fled. When she was turned into a zombie soon after, part of her was glad. It meant she wouldn't have to live with her shame and guilt.

But B had been injected with a secret vaccine when she was a child. It gave her the ability to fight the zombie gene and regain her senses. Death was not the end for Miss Smith.

After a spell of captivity in an underground complex run by the army, B escaped and wound her way across London. She found temporary shelter with an artist who lived in an old brewery on Brick Lane. Later she crossed paths with the homicidal clown, Mr Dowling, and Owl Man, a bizarre-looking individual with the largest eyes she had ever seen.

B was eventually offered refuge by Dr Oystein, a century-old zombie who was leading the fight to restore order to the world. He claimed to be a servant of God, given a heavenly mandate to combat the forces of darkness. He had assembled a team of conscious, revitalised zombies and christened them Angels.

Wary of Dr Oystein and his religious beliefs, B left his base in County Hall. Returning to the studio of her artist friend, Timothy, she discovered him nursing an eerie, genderless baby with hellish eyes. She had dreamt of babies like this when she was alive. It even spoke the same way that the babies in her nightmares had.

There was a spike through the baby's head. When B removed it, the baby shrieked and summoned a horde of zombies from the streets. They killed Timothy and took the baby away. Before it departed, it asked B to come with them, but she wanted nothing to do with the monstrous infant.

After she'd buried Timothy, B made her way back to County Hall and pledged herself to Dr Oystein and his cause. She was now willing to grant him the benefit of the doubt, seeing the baby from her dreams as possible evidence that this was a world of mysterious, godly influence.

B trained hard with the other Angels. She didn't trust them all – especially a thug called Rage, who had betrayed her in the underground complex – and spurned their offers of friendship, not wanting to get close to anyone after she had lost so many friends and relatives.

One day, while on a scouting mission, she was kidnapped by a living hunter. He delivered her to the Board, a group of powerful tyrants who made her fight and kill other zombies. B seemed doomed until Dr Oystein and his Angels boarded the ship and set her free. When she saw how they had risked their lives to help her, she put her misgivings aside and committed herself totally to the cause. She had at last found a true home, and friends to share it with.

NOW . . .

ONE

ONE

I'm in Timothy's gallery, the Old Truman Brewery, on Brick Lane. It's quiet and cool. Daylight filters through the cracks in the boards covering the windows.

The last thing Timothy asked, before he was killed by a mob of zombies, was that I take care of his paintings. He thought he had been given a commission by God, that it was his duty to record the downfall of London, so that future generations could study his pictures of this terrible time and learn from them.

Timothy was mad as a hatter but he was a nice guy. I feel like I owe him, since I was the one who set free the grisly baby who called the zombies down upon him, so I've come here several times since he died, to dump the food he had stocked up, wash the bloodstains from the floor and generally make sure that everything is in order.

There are hundreds of paintings stacked against the walls, spread throughout the various rooms. Some are hanging too. I rotate the pictures on display whenever I come, swapping them round, choosing new examples from the many on offer. I think Timothy would have liked that.

I'm holding one of the paintings, studying it critically, trying to decide whether or not it deserves a spot on the wall. It's a painting of a zombie tucking into the skull of a dead woman. It must have been dangerous for Timothy, getting that close, but he was always reckless. Anything to get a good angle.

A wild flower sprouts from a crack in the pavement close to the dead woman's head. It's more brightly coloured than the corpse or the zombie, its

petals painted in glorious yellows and pinks. The flower makes this painting stand out, but at the same time it makes it look a bit arty-farty. I'm sure the flower was real – Timothy only painted what he saw – but because of the way he's highlighted it, it doesn't *look* real.

I know I'm being silly, hesitating like this. Nobody's going to pass through here any time soon. I'm Timothy's only audience, and probably will continue to be for many years to come. It makes no difference whether I give this pride of place on a wall or jam it behind a load of other paintings.

Still, it matters to me. I never paid much attention to art when I was alive, but I've been getting into it since I settled in at County Hall. I've spent much of my free time scouring galleries and reading about the history of art. It's become an interesting hobby, a way of keeping boredom at bay when I'm not training with the other Angels.

I've no artistic talent, but arranging Timothy's paintings is a way for me to creatively express myself. So I study the painting with the flower one last time, forehead creased as if I'm attempting to crack a difficult puzzle. Finally I snort and return it to the pile, at least for the time being. I might grant it wall space in the future, but not today.

As I'm carefully slotting the painting back into place, there's a loud thumping sound on the staircase behind me.

I whirl and adopt a defensive position. I flex my fingers, getting ready to slash with the bones sticking out of them if I'm attacked. I don't have a heart, not since it was ripped from my chest, but my mind remembers what anxiety was like when I was alive, and I imagine the sound of my quickening heartbeat inside my head.

I don't call out. I don't move. I just stand silently and wait.

There's another thumping noise, this time closer to the top of the stairs. I grit my teeth and suppress a shiver. Zombies don't scare me. Nor do the living. But this could be Mr Dowling, Owl Man or that nightmarish baby. Maybe it sniffed me out and returned to finish the job. It let me go when it was here before. Maybe it changed its mind and came back to send me the way of poor Timothy.

Another thump, this one almost at the very top stair. I frown. By now I should be able to see whoever is making the noise. But there's no sign of anyone.

The silence stretches out. Then someone moans my name.

'*Beckyyyyyy . . .*'

I growl softly and relax. 'You think you're clever, don't you?'

'I don't think it,' comes the cheerful response. 'I know it!'

Then Rage stands up from where he had been lying on the stairs and grins at me. I shoot him the finger and go back to appraising the paintings, trying to act as if the annoying hulk isn't here, hiding my relief, not wanting him to know that he really did spook me. Admit to being scared? Not in this unlife! And definitely not to a cynical, bullying piece of trash like Rage. I'd rather claw out my own eyes than give that creep the satisfaction of knowing how close he'd come to making a dead girl shiver.

TWO

'Aren't you surprised to see me?' Rage asks when I continue to ignore him.

'Nothing about you surprises me,' I sniff.

'Don't you want to know how I found you?' he presses.

'I'm guessing you followed me from County Hall.'

Rage chuckles and scratches the hole in his left cheek where he was bitten by a zombie when he was turned. Wisps of green moss sprout from it, like the world's worst designer beard.

'Don't flatter yourself,' Rage says. 'I wouldn't waste my time following the likes of you.'

'Yet here you are . . .' I purr.

'I'm not alone,' he says. 'My partner wanted to check this place out.'

'What poor sap is lonely and desperate enough to hang out with you?' I sneer as someone else comes up the stairs behind Rage. Then I spot who it is and wince. 'Mr Burke. I'm sorry. I didn't mean to slag you off.'

Billy Burke waves away my apology. 'If I'd known you were here, I wouldn't have disturbed you. But we were passing and I remembered you telling me about this place. I was keen to see the paintings. We can leave if you'd prefer to be alone.'

'No, that's OK, come in. I'll give you the grand tour.'

Burke used to be my biology teacher. He was the best we had in our school, one of the few teachers I respected. He also saw the real me long before I did. He told me I was heading down the same racist path as my dad, warned me that I needed to change. I ignored him. Back then I thought I knew myself better than anybody else did.

I've often wondered how things might have turned out if I'd listened to him. Maybe I wouldn't have thrown poor Tyler Bayor to the zombies. Maybe I'd have survived the zombie apocalypse. Maybe I wouldn't be spending my nights staring at the ceiling, thinking about the blood I have on my hands, wishing I was truly dead.

Burke hooked up with Dr Oystein after London fell and worked as a spy in the underground complex where I was being held when I recovered my senses. That's where we met again. He convinced the soldiers to feed me brains to keep my senses intact. I'd be a mindless killer zombie if not for his help. He saw something in me worth fighting for. Even though I thought I was worthless, he didn't agree, and he did all that he could to save me and steer me right.

In an ideal world, if we were able to choose our parents, I'd pick Billy Burke for my father without a second's hesitation. Not that I'll ever tell him that, or even hint at it. I don't want him thinking I'm a soppy git.

I show Burke round the gallery. He's fascinated by the paintings, though he finds some of them hard to look at—the living are far more sensitive about these things than the undead. Rage is less impressed and keeps yawning behind Burke's back, trying to wind me up. I treat him with the contempt he deserves and don't even reward him with another flash of my finger.

'There are so many,' Burke murmurs after a while, shaking his head at the piles of paintings resting against the walls. 'He must have painted like a machine.'

'Yeah,' I nod. 'It was his entire life. He knew his time would probably be cut short, so he crammed in as much as he could.'

'Have you looked at them all?' Burke asks.

'Most of them, though there are still a few buried away in places that I haven't got to yet.'

'And did he arrange the paintings on the walls or have you hung them?'

I fight a proud smile. 'He hung a lot of them, but I've been switching them and alternating the display.'

'Are you looking to get a job as a curator?' Rage asks sweetly.

'Get stuffed,' I snap.

Burke makes a shushing gesture. 'This collection is quite something, B,' he says. 'Thank you for sharing it with us.'

'Any time,' I tell him happily. 'But what were you doing out this way in the first place? And with Rage, of all people.'

'What's wrong with me?' Rage barks, taking a step towards me, his beady eyes glinting in the dim light.

'Easy,' Burke soothes him. 'I'd have thought that the pair of you would have settled your differences by now.'

'It's hard to settle your differences with a guy who pushes you off the London Eye,' I snarl.

Rage cackles. 'You're not still sore about that, are you?'

'I'll return the favour sometime,' I jeer. 'See how long it takes you to forget.'

Rage fakes a sigh and pulls a wounded expression.

19

'See how she baits me, sir? Some people just can't find forgiveness within themselves.'

'Grow up, Michael,' Burke says witheringly, using Rage's real name to show his annoyance. Then he stares at me. 'I thought you fell off the Eye.'

I wince, remembering I hadn't told anyone what really happened up there. It's no big secret. I just didn't want people thinking I was a grass. I can deal with my own problems.

'That's right,' I mumble. 'I did fall.'

Burke frowns and starts to ask a question. Then he shakes his head. 'Not my business,' he says and goes back down the stairs. Rage scowls at me, then trails after Burke. I follow.

There's a trolley on the ground floor, stacked high with folders and files. Burke nods at them. 'That's why we were passing. I've been researching something. The records I'm interested in don't seem to have ever been transferred to computer, so I've had to track down hard copies. I finally found them in a building north of here. It's a place where a secretive branch of the army used to keep their paperwork, one of a number of hiding-holes scattered around the city. I got the addresses when I was working for Josh Massoglia and I've been checking them out. Most of the buildings have been gutted, but this one seems to have been overlooked. I spent a few days gathering the documents I was after and asked Rage to help me transport them back to County Hall, so that I could go through them in my spare time.'

'You should have asked me,' I frown. 'I'd have helped.'

'I know,' Burke smiles. 'But the files are heavy. I needed a brute with lots of muscles.'

'And they don't come more brute than me,' Rage says, puffing himself up.

'What are you looking for?' I ask.

'Probably nothing important,' Burke says. 'I just have an itch I need to scratch. You know what it's like when something bugs you and you can't let it drop?'

'Yeah. Do you want a hand going through the files?'

'It's kind of you to offer, but no, I'd rather do it myself. As I said, I doubt it's important, so I don't want to waste anybody's time other than my own.'

'It'll take you months to plough through that lot,' I note.

'No,' he says. 'I know what I'm looking for. I'll be able to skim through the pages pretty quickly. But maybe you can help push the trolley. Rage was starting to struggle.'

'No I wasn't,' Rage shouts, then catches Burke's grin and relaxes.

Burke turns to leave, then spots a painting hanging on a nearby wall and stalls. It's one of the most disturbing pictures in the gallery. I gave it a wall to itself, even though it's not a large canvas.

The crazed clown, Mr Dowling, dominates the painting. Timothy captured him in all his finery, the v-shaped gouges cut through the flesh of his face from his eyes down to his mouth, the pinstripe suit, severed faces pinned to his shoulders, lengths of gut wound round his arms, clumps of hair stapled to his skull.

Owl Man is nearby, with his pot belly, white hair, pale skin and those incredibly large eyes. There are also several mutants, with their rotting skin and yellow eyes, wearing hoodies.

Burke edges closer to the painting as if mesmerised. Rage stumbles after him, looking every bit as sombre. The pair stop in front of it and stare in silence.

'Is that Mr Dowling?' Rage asks.

'No,' I grunt. 'It's Santa Claus.'

'I've heard him described, but I never thought . . .' Rage falls silent again.

'Do you believe Dr Oystein now?' Burke asks softly. 'When he says that Mr Dowling is an agent of universal evil?'

Rage shifts uncomfortably. 'Do you?' He throws the question back.

Burke breathes out slowly. 'I still find it hard to believe in a God or Devil who would get personally involved in our affairs. But when I look at that, I wonder.'

'You've met this guy a couple of times?' Rage asks, turning towards me.

'Yeah. Underground in the complex, and when he brought down a helicopter in Trafalgar Square.'

'Is he as creepy in the flesh?'

'Way more,' I say shortly.

'What about the freak with the eyes?' Rage asks.

'I just know him as Owl Man. Dr Oystein knows his real name, but he –'

'What makes you think that?' Burke interrupts.

'He told me.'

'Did he tell you what it was?' Burke asks.

'No. He said he preferred the name Owl Man and would call him that from now on.'

Burke grunts. 'I must quiz him when I get back. *Owl Man* is one of the people I'm hoping to learn more about in the files.'

'Why?' Rage asks. 'Do you want to send him a birthday card?'

We all laugh and the mood lightens.

'It's some world we live in, isn't it?' Burke sighs.

'Imagine if you'd had to dissect something like Mr Dowling in a biology class,' I giggle.

'Maybe I'll get a chance yet,' Burke says, turning back towards the trolley. Then he pauses thoughtfully and looks around. 'Would you mind if I did some of my research here?'

I shrug. 'If you want.'

'I wouldn't be in your way?'

'No. I was about done. I can go get you a chair.'

'That's OK. I'm used to doing it on my feet.'

Rage and I smirk at the unintended joke.

'Will he be safe here?' Rage asks me.

'Should be. Timothy got along fine until that bloody baby started screeching. The windows are boarded over – I replaced most of the planks that were broken – and I've made sure all the doors are properly barred. But what about getting back to County Hall?'

'Thank you for your concern, but I *am* able to look after myself,' Burke says with a hint of irritation. 'I managed to negotiate the streets of London for months without any help before you two came along to nanny me.'

'But it wouldn't hurt to have one of us with you, would it?' I ask him.

Burke grimaces. 'I'm not a child. Now get the hell out of here before I revive the custom of detention.'

Rage and I laugh. 'OK,' I tell my old teacher. 'The

key's in the door. Lock up after yourself and leave it under the stone out front.'

'If you're not back by sunset, should we come looking for you?' Rage asks.

'Give it until sunset tomorrow,' Burke tells him, eyeing the tower of files and folders. 'I'm going to be here a while with that lot. I'll work late into the night, sleep in, then hit the pile again when I wake up. If I can get through it all, it will save us having to push the trolley any further. I worry about getting attacked out on the streets, going slowly with a load like that.'

'There's no food, but the taps work,' I tell him. 'Or they did the last time I checked. We could bring you some grub and bottled water.'

'A bit of fasting will do me no harm,' Burke says and shoos us out. He's grinning when he waves us off, but I catch him staring at the painting of Mr Dowling as he shuts the door. His smile disappears as the shadow of the closing door sweeps across him, and sorrow and fear eclipse him in one smooth, sliding motion.

THREE

Rage and I head west to County Hall. It used to be the seat of local government years ago. Now it's home to Dr Oystein and his Angels, a place for us to train and prepare for battle with Mr Dowling and his troops.

We don't say anything for a while. I don't like Rage and he's no fonder of me. We share a room with four other revitaliseds, and manage to be pleasant to one another most of the time, but I can never truly forgive him for what he did in the underground complex, when he abandoned me and the zom heads.

Rage breaks the silence. 'You looked sharp in training yesterday.'

I squint at him suspiciously.

'What?' he asks.

'You don't pay compliments for the hell of it,' I snap. 'What do you want?'

Rage rolls his eyes. 'You know your problem, *Becky*? You're paranoid.'

'Only where you're concerned,' I snarl.

Rage laughs. 'Out of all the do-gooders in County Hall, you're the most like me. It's a shame you hate my guts. We could have been like Bonnie and Clyde if the circumstances were different.'

'More like Burke and Hare,' I mutter.

'Who were they?'

'A couple of grave-robbers.'

Rage smiles. 'You say the sweetest things.'

We walk along in silence a bit more until Rage speaks up again. 'Seriously, you did look sharp in training, and no, I'm not after anything. I'm just saying. You've been on fire since you came back from HMS *Belfast*.'

I shrug. 'Yeah, well, when you have to fight as a gladiator several times a day you either toughen up or get ripped to pieces.'

It's been nearly four months since I was held captive on the old cruiser. I spent several weeks in a Groove Tube when I got back, recovering, my wounds slowly knitting together as much as they were able to. Since then I've been working tirelessly with Master Zhang, developing my skills.

'When do you think the doc will send us on a real mission?' Rage asks.

'What am I, a mind-reader?'

'It had better be soon,' Rage grumbles. 'I'm getting bored of this crap. There's only so much training and scouting that I can take. I'm starting to crack up.'

'You cracked up long ago,' I sniff, then cock an eyebrow at him. 'I don't think anyone likes being stuck in County Hall, but what can we do? Dr Oystein calls the shots. When he thinks we're ready, he'll set us loose. Until then . . .'

Rage shoots me a dirty look. 'The others in our team were sent on serious missions before we joined, so he obviously trusts them to do a job for him. It's you and me he's unsure of.'

'Maybe,' I nod. 'Or maybe he's holding us back for something big.'

'Like what?' Rage asks. 'The ultimate confrontation with Mr Dowling and the forces of darkness?'

'Perhaps.'

Rage snorts. 'That's never gonna happen. It's a load of bull, God, the Devil, all the rest. The doc needs the clown and his mutants to keep the game going. That's why we haven't squared up to them. If we faced them and beat them, we'd see that they were just a bunch of dirty rotten creeps. He'll never pit us against Mr Dowling. The two of them are probably drinking buddies.'

I stop and stare at him. 'You don't really believe that.'

'I do,' he says. 'Well, not the drinking buddies bit, but the rest of it, yeah. I've been sizing up the mad old geezer. I like the doc, but the whole good versus evil thing bothered me from the start, and the more I've seen of him and the way he's holding us back, the more my opinion has changed.

'I used to think he was crazy, that he believes

everything he preaches. Now I'm not so sure. I think he knows that it's nonsense. That's why he doesn't lead us into battle with the mutants. If he does, and we win, he'll have to admit the truth once the fighting's died down, that he's just a normal zombie, with no more of a role to play in deciding the future of this world than anyone else.'

'What if everything he's told us is on the level?' I ask quietly. 'If he really *is* an agent of a higher power? If Mr Dowling really does represent some force of ultimate evil?'

Rage sneers. 'You're smarter than that. You know it's bullshit.'

'No,' I whisper. 'I used to think it was. Now . . .'

I start walking again, picking up speed. Rage hurries after me.

'Is this because of the baby?' he asks. 'You were sure the doc was psycho before you went to the brewery. When you came back, you were a convert. What went down?'

'There's no point telling you. You wouldn't believe me.'

'I might,' he huffs.

'Not in a million years.' I squint at him. 'It's funny. After you pushed me off the London Eye, you told me I had to choose, that I needed to pledge myself to Dr Oystein or get the hell out of London. Now you're the one caught in two minds.'

'Caught? Me?' He laughs at the notion. 'I'm clear on where I stand. I think the doc's a hero. He'd sacrifice more than any of us ever would. But I don't buy into his holy war. I think he's bigged up the threat of Mr Dowling in order to fool himself into thinking he's on a mission from God. He should have led us into battle by now and wiped out the mutants, so we could link up with the army and focus on the problem of clearing the city of zombies.

'But he doesn't want to do that, not deep down. He says he plans to hand control of the planet back to the living again, but I think secretly he prefers it like this. He can tell himself he's important this way. If we fight the mutants and eliminate them, but the world rolls on the same as before, what's he then?'

'If that's how you feel, what are you doing here?' I

ask. 'Why don't you do us all a favour and bugger off?'

'I'm thinking about it,' he says. 'The main reason I've hung around is the promise of an exciting battle—I still think there could be a good old dust-up between the Angels and mutants, and I've been hanging on for that. But if he doesn't give us something to do soon, I'll look for action elsewhere.'

'Good riddance,' I tell him.

Rage's smile returns. 'You don't mean that. You'd miss me if I went.'

'In your dreams.'

'No,' he says. 'You would. That's why I'm inviting you to come with me.'

I gawp at him. 'Are you crazy? I hate you. What makes you think I'd give up County Hall and turn my back on the friends I've made, to be your side-kick?'

'Because you're itching for action too,' Rage says. 'You're sick of the quiet life. You want to be in the thick of things, like you were on the *Belfast*. You need action, fighting, killing. Tell me I'm wrong.'

'You're wrong,' I spit back at him immediately.

Rage shakes his head smugly and jogs ahead of me, leaving me to stare after him and seethe. Me and Rage, two of the same? Never in a million years!

At least . . . I don't think that we are.

God, I *hope* we're not!

FOUR

Some of the Angels are playing football in Jubilee
Gardens when I get back. The small park is nestled
between County Hall and the Royal Festival Hall,
where they used to host shows, concerts and high-
brow events.

I spot Shane passing the ball to Jakob, so I stop to
cheer them on. I was never a huge footie fan, but I
can tolerate it.

I join Ashtat on the sidelines. We didn't gel when
we first met, but we get on fine now. She's wearing
her usual blue robe, but has replaced her white head-
scarf with a red one.

'That's new,' I note.

'I fancied a change.' She smiles shyly. 'Do you think the colour suits me?'

'Yeah, it's nice.'

She beams. 'The boys said they liked it, but they know nothing about fashion. I was waiting for a girl to give me her opinion.'

I scratch the back of my head. I'm not a girly girl. I grew up a tomboy and preferred hanging out with guys. I always shaved my hair tight, wore trousers and T-shirts, no earrings or jewellery. I fought like a boy, cursed like a boy, acted like a boy. It feels strange being asked for advice about something like this. The girls who I was friendly with in school never sounded me out about clothes, hair or make-up.

'Good tackle, Shane,' I roar, focusing my attention on the football. 'What's the score?'

'A couple of goals apiece,' Ashtat says. 'At least I think so. The game started before I got here.'

We watch the match unfold. There are nine play-ers on either side. They found proper football nets somewhere and set them up. Shane, Carl, Jakob and

Rage are on one team. Rage must have replaced someone just before I got back. He plays dirty, going in high with his tackles, elbowing players off the ball. No surprise there.

The ghostly white Jakob gets the ball and speeds down the wing. He looks so frail compared with the others, a result of the cancer which was eating away at him when he was alive. But zombies are tough, even the weakest of us, and Jakob can more than hold his own.

The game flows swiftly, faster than it ever did in the Premier League. Fully fed zombies are stronger and quicker than they were in life. We don't need oxygen, so we don't run out of breath or tire rapidly. Any of these players could shoot from one end of the pitch and expect to rattle the back of the net in the goal at the far end if their shot was on target.

Jakob passes to Carl, who fires off a close-range, blistering shot. The keeper throws himself low and left and scoops the ball away just before it crosses the line. Carl cries out with disbelief and kicks the ground angrily, sending a clod of earth flying through the air. Ashtat and I laugh at him, then roar encouragement.

The other team breaks. The players swarm up the pitch and score. One of the guys on our side groans and limps off, but only his pride has really been injured.

'Fancy a game, B?' Carl calls.

'I'm useless,' I shout back.

'So are we,' he laughs. 'Come on, we need a woman's subtle touch.'

'Do you fancy it?' I ask Ashtat.

She shakes her head. 'I am not dressed for football.'

'What are you scared of?' Rage yells.

I glower at Rage then roll up my sleeves. 'Right. Time to show you mugs what the beautiful game's all about.'

To a chorus of cheers from my room-mates I take to the pitch.

I wasn't lying when I said that I was useless. Well, not completely. I can do the basics—pass, shoot, tackle and run with the ball. I just can't do any of

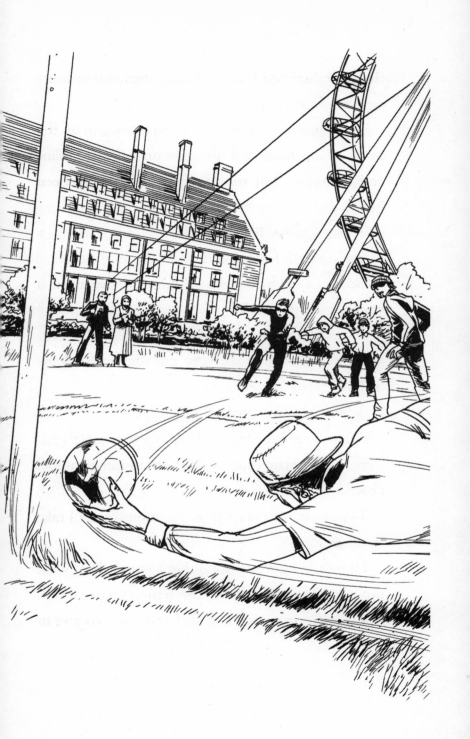

them very well. Fortunately for me, most of the other Angels are pretty crap too, so I don't feel completely out of place.

My guys watch out for me. When I'm bundled over by one of the larger members of the opposition, Shane and Carl sandwich him soon after, slamming into him at the same time from either side, to teach him a lesson. It's sweet of them, but they didn't need to. I can exact my own revenge, as I prove the next time I cross paths with the big guy—I slyly punch him below the belt when no one's looking, then claim total innocence when he screeches and protests.

'I saw what you did,' Jakob says quietly as I move away from the argument.

'He deserved it,' I snort.

'I'm not saying he didn't. But hitting a guy between the legs isn't as effective as it used to be. Elbow one of his ears next time. That will *really* hurt him.'

I laugh and we knock knuckles.

A couple of minutes later I almost score a goal when I mishit a pass from Rage. Their keeper pulls off another spectacular save, otherwise it would have been a dead cert. Ashtat cheers loudly from the side-line and tells me she's sure I'll score next time.

'Nice one, shrimp,' Rage says, slapping my back as he jogs past. 'Keep it up.'

I grin like an idiot, feeling way better than I should playing such a stupid game, especially when there's nothing at stake. But it feels good to be kicking a ball around, part of a team, playing with friends. It's been a long time since I felt like this, that I truly belonged.

The game trundles along aimlessly. Nobody's worried about how long we've been playing or the score or when we're going to stop. We're just having fun, stuck in a deliciously vague, carefree moment, the kind you wish could last forever but never does.

The twins shatter the mood. Cian and Awnya are the youngest Angels, great at foraging—they can find just about anything you want. They come racing out of County Hall, eager as a pair of hounds after a hare. Awnya starts waving her hands over her head to stop the game even before they reach the pitch. 'Carl!' she cries. 'Shane! B!'

'Rage!' Cian adds. 'Jakob! Ashtat!'

'What is it?' Shane grunts, picking up the ball and bouncing it hard on the spot, letting the twins know that they can expect him to bounce it off their heads if they haven't halted the game for an excellent reason.

'Dr Oystein wants you,' Awnya exclaims.

'You're going on a mission,' Cian says. Then his face drops. 'I wish we could come with you.'

As the others punch the air with excitement, I catch Rage's eye. He shrugs. 'Sod's law,' he chuckles. 'If I hadn't thought about leaving, we would never have been given a mission. As soon as I think about upping sticks, destiny hits us with a wallop. It's always the way, isn't it?'

Shane kicks the ball high into the air and leaves the other players to chase it. Ashtat joins the rest of us on the pitch. We glance around at each other and share a buzzing yet nervously charged moment. Then we head on back to County Hall with the twins to find out what fate holds in store.

FIVE

Dr Oystein is in one of the rooms overlooking the river and the Houses of Parliament. It's a stunning view but he's not paying attention to it. He's sitting in a chair, bent over a map on a small table. Master Zhang is discussing something with him.

Emma and Declan, a pair of living humans, are also present. We chanced upon them before I was kidnapped by Barnes and taken to HMS *Belfast*. They came to live here while I was being held prisoner. Emma is bouncing Declan up and down on her lap. He's smiling but he doesn't laugh out loud.

He hasn't said anything since she brought him here. He's the quietest little boy I've ever met. I suppose silence is a useful tool when you're trying to stay alive on the zombie-infested streets.

The twins leave us and Dr Oystein settles back in his chair. 'Well, I think you all know why you are here.'

'A mission,' Shane yelps, clenching his right hand into a fist – but not closing it all the way, because of the bones sticking out of the tips – and shaking it.

'It should not excite you,' Master Zhang frowns. 'This is a serious business, not a game. Perhaps we should assign this task to one of the other groups.'

As Shane's face falls, Dr Oystein smiles. 'Take no notice of Zhang. He has a dry sense of humour. We understand how frustrating life is for you, stuck here, training so hard. Your excitement is understandable and I am confident you will put it to one side and focus on the mission once the initial, thrilling flush has passed.

'Now for specifics.' He waves a hand at the humans. 'The reason I have chosen you for this mission is that it involves Emma and Declan. They have been happy here, but it is time for them to move on.'

'We're not ungrateful,' Emma says. 'I just think it would be healthier for Declan to be with other children . . . other living children I mean.' She blushes as she says it and looks away.

'No need to feel guilty,' Dr Oystein says sweetly. 'We would all want the same thing for him in your position. We would have sent you with the children from the cruiser if he had not been ill at the time.'

One of the creeps on the *Belfast* – the despicable Dan-Dan – kept a bunch of children below deck to torture and kill. Angels took those we rescued to stay in compounds in the countryside. Declan caught a bug shortly before they were due to leave. He was vomiting and coughing. Dr Oystein considered postponing the exodus of children, but Emma didn't want them to be put at risk on her son's account. She insisted they depart as scheduled and has been waiting here since. She hasn't put any pressure on the doctor, refusing to accept his offer of a private escort out of the city.

'A couple of our Angels recently discovered a small group of people sheltering in a building in Hammersmith,' Dr Oystein says. 'We are going to lead them to a place beyond the city limits, where they can join a community of other survivors. I would like you to escort Emma and Declan to Hammersmith, then travel with the group to the compound.'

'We're getting out of London?' Carl asks, his face lighting up.

'For a while, yes.' Dr Oystein stands, looks briefly out of the window, then faces us again. 'Do not underestimate the dangers of this mission. Other zombies leave you alone when you are by yourselves, but they will not ignore you when they catch the scent of fresh brains. You will have to move swiftly and cautiously, and you will almost surely be called upon to fight.

'You might also come under attack from living forces. The city and countryside are full of angry, bitter people who are trying to execute as many of the undead as they can. They will not distinguish

46

between a revitalised and a revived. Most do not know that there is a difference. And most would not care.

'It is a hostile, threatening environment, and I would like each one of you to think carefully about it before deciding whether or not to accept this assignment. No,' he adds as Rage starts to speak. 'I do not want your answer now. Rest on the matter overnight and give it serious consideration. If you accept, you will not have to leave until morning. You can let me know your verdict then.'

The others file out of the room, trying to act sombre, even though they're wild with glee inside. There's not a chance that any of them will turn down this opportunity to get out of the city. But I suppose we have to go through the motions to keep Dr Oystein happy.

I don't retire with the rest of my group. I want to ask the doc something. He sees that I have a question and nods for me to stay behind as Zhang, Emma and Declan slip out. He sits in his chair again and beckons me forward.

'How have you been?' he asks.

'Fine.'

The doc hasn't been here a lot over the last few weeks. He has a secret lab somewhere, and spends a lot of his time there, working on ways to wipe out the undead hordes.

'I wanted to ask you about the babies,' I mutter. 'You haven't said anything about them since you got back.'

Dr Oystein makes a small sighing noise. 'There is not much that I can tell you at the moment. There are things I am considering. I do not like to keep secrets, but it is a case of deciding how much information I think it is fitting to share with you – or any of the other Angels – right now.'

He crosses his legs and studies me closely. 'I am still troubled by the fact that you dreamt of the babies when you were alive, and that Owl Man knew of your dreams. I have been researching ways in which I might induce a sleep-like state in a revitalised.'

I frown. 'I thought we could never sleep again.'

'I thought so too,' Dr Oystein says. 'And that may well be the case. It is not something I ever gave much thought to, since it seemed a trivial issue. But I would be keen to find out if you could still have the dreams, and if we could learn anything from them.

'I have started to experiment. It might lead nowhere, and even if it does, there is no way of telling how long it will take before I am successful. But if I can find a way to make you sleep, would you be prepared to brave your nightmares again in an attempt to explore them further?'

'I would if you'll tell me what you know about the babies,' I reply.

'That sounds like a fair deal,' he smiles. 'I promise to reveal all before you agree to any tests, assuming we get that far.'

Dr Oystein stands and stretches. 'Come, I am heading to my laboratory here, and I would like you to accompany me some of the way.'

I fall in beside him. 'You know, if you can find a way for me to sleep, the other Angels will want to snooze too. Time drags when we're awake all night.

This could be one of your more popular inventions, up there with the Groove Tubes.'

'You think so?' Dr Oystein looks surprised. 'I had not realised it was that important. I know lack of sleep is a nuisance, but I had not thought it a serious handicap. Perhaps I should have turned my mind to the matter sooner. I will give it all of the attention that I can over the next few –'

'*Demon!*' someone screams and we both jump with alarm.

I look up and spot Mr Burke in the corridor. He has a face like thunder and he's holding a gun. As I stare at him, bewildered, he bellows '*Demon!*' again. Then he raises the gun, aims at us and opens fire.

SIX

Dr Oystein and I throw ourselves to opposite sides of the corridor. It's what I was taught to do by Master Zhang in a situation like this. It means the gunman has to swivel and set his sights on just one person.

Burke focuses on Dr Oystein. He keeps firing as he strides forward, screaming '*Demon!*' over and over, as if it's the only word he knows.

'Stop!' I roar, racing towards him, waving my arms, trying to draw him away from Dr Oystein. The doc is dodging the bullets as best he can, moving with surprising speed for a guy his age.

Burke ignores me and keeps on firing. His eyes are wild. Spit flies from his lips every time he roars. Even in the heat of the moment I feel a stab of envy. You can't produce proper spit when you're a zombie. My mouth has been a dry, stale hole ever since I came back to life.

I close on Burke and he swings his arm round. He starts to fire, but pauses when he sees that it's me. A desperate expression shoots across his face. He adjusts his aim slightly and shoots at the floor ahead of me, trying to scare me off.

But I don't scare easily. I keep on coming. Burke's features harden and he whirls away, closer to the wall, searching for a clear shot at Dr Oystein. He fires again. There's a cry of pain as one of the bullets strikes home. I don't look back to check on the doc. There isn't time.

'Stop!' I yell again as I come within striking distance of the man who was once my favourite teacher.

'*Demon!*' Burke retorts, steadying his arm, taking careful aim.

I want to calm him down and talk this through,

but there's no time. If I don't stop him, he's going to kill Dr Oystein. In a panic, I swing at his gun hand and swat the weapon away. Burke cries out with pain and stumbles after his lost weapon. Then he comes to a halt and stares at the fingers which a second before had been holding the gun.

I pulled my punch as much as I could. I knew the dangers of direct contact and tried to avoid it, so that I could subdue Burke and try to find out what's wrong with him. But you can't always strike accurately in a fight, not when your opponent has a gun and is about to kill one of your team.

I knocked the gun from Burke's hand. But a couple of the bones sticking out of my fingers scratched his palm.

Burke stares at the wounds, his eyes bulging. They're minor scrapes. A kitten could have done more damage. But Burke hasn't been scratched by a cat. He's been scratched by a zombie. And the infectious nick of a monster like me is death to a human like him.

'I'm sorry!' I scream, thrusting my hands behind my back, as if I can undo what I've done. 'I didn't mean to. I only wanted to knock away the gun. Why didn't you stop firing when I told you?'

Burke stares at me, his cheeks puffing in and out. There are tears in his eyes. He clutches the injured hand to his chest and falls to his knees. Shakes his head and moans pitifully.

Master Zhang races into the corridor, followed by some Angels. His eyes dart from Burke to me to Dr Oystein, taking in everything in an instant. 'Are you in control of the situation?' he barks.

I can't answer.

'Becky Smith!' he snaps. 'Are you in control?'

'Yes,' I say hoarsely, my training kicking in as I take a firmer stance, ready to stop Burke if he makes another grab for the gun.

'Oystein,' Zhang shouts, racing past me. 'Are you injured?'

'Only winged,' Dr Oystein says. 'One of the bullets struck my shoulder. I will be all right.'

I don't look back. I stay focused on Burke. He's crying openly now. He holds out his injured hand to me and whispers something.

'What was that?' I moan, expecting him to say '*Demon!*' again. But this time it's different.

'*Dowling,*' Burke croaks through his tears, and I go cold inside as I start to piece together what has happened.

I sit beside the damned Billy Burke, the man who saved me in the underground complex, who has helped take care of me since I came to County Hall, who was always a good friend and trusted teacher, the man I would have chosen for a father if I could. I wrap my arms round him and pull him close, like a mother nursing her baby.

'It's OK,' I tell him as he starts to quiver uncontrollably. 'I'm with you. I'll look out for you. It won't be long now. The pain will pass.'

'Dowling,' Burke says again, sobbing into the fabric of my T-shirt.

'I know,' I shush him. 'Don't worry. I'll track him down. I'll make that bastard pay.'

Burke starts shaking his head and tries to say something else. But before he can, his body rattles. His head flies back and his eyelids snap open and shut, time and time again. There's a creaking noise as the bones in his fingers and toes start to push out, tearing through the flesh. His lips peel back as his teeth lengthen and thicken into fangs.

Master Zhang returns and stands over the pair of us. He looks furious but sad at the same time. I don't know if he was friends with Burke – I'm not sure that Zhang has any real friends – but he respected the ex-teacher.

I clutch Burke tight and whisper in his ear, trying to make this as comfortable for him as I can, even though I know his brain has already shut down, that he can't understand anything I'm saying.

'B,' Zhang says quietly. I glance up at him. He extends his right hand, the fingers hooked, and raises a questioning eyebrow, asking if I want him to put the transforming human out of his misery.

I start to nod, then recall something and shake my head, angry at myself for almost forgetting such a crucial factor. 'No! He got Dr Oystein to vaccinate him. He wanted the chance of revitalising if he was ever infected.'

'There is little hope of that,' Zhang says icily. 'Adults almost never revitalise. And after what he did today, I am not sure he deserves such consideration.'

I think about defending Burke, but I know that won't wash with my stern mentor. So I take a sly approach instead. 'As unlikely as it is, if he recovers consciousness, we can find out why he did this, punish whoever put him up to it.'

Zhang purses his lips, thinks about that, then nods curtly. 'I will prepare a room and we will keep him captive. Guard him until it is ready—I do not want him to target Ciara or Reilly.'

As Zhang turns to check on Dr Oystein, Burke falls impossibly still. Impossible if you're a human, that is. Perfectly possible if you're a zombie.

Burke tries to rise but I pull him down. He doesn't resist. While Master Zhang and the other Angels tend to Dr Oystein, I gently rock the undead teacher and go on speaking to him, mourning his loss while at the same time begging his forgiveness for having been the one who killed him.

SEVEN

Dr Oystein waves away Master Zhang's help and rushes down the corridor, calling his Angels to arms, demanding all entrances be secured and the building searched for intruders. I remain with Burke's revived corpse as everyone else races round in a panic. Nobody's sure if there's an army outside, ready to break down the doors, or if Burke acted by himself.

Finally the doctor and Master Zhang return. Dr Oystein hasn't changed clothes or bandaged his wound. There's a small web of thick blood spreading slowly from a hole in his left shoulder. He winces as he squats beside me, but otherwise ignores his injury.

'I am sorry,' he says softly as he examines the newly created zombie. 'Billy was a good man. He deserved better than this.'

'He was vaccinated,' I remind the doctor. 'He might revitalise.'

'I will pray for him,' Dr Oystein says. 'And we will guard him safely and keep him fed and comfortable.'

'For how long?' I ask.

'As long as you wish,' he says, then gently prises Burke away from me and helps him to his feet. As the zombie looks around blankly, Dr Oystein asks one of the Angels to take him to a nearby room and lock him away. 'We will sort out more fitting accommodation for him later,' he vows.

'What the hell happened?' Zhang snarls as the walking dead teacher is led away. 'Why did he want to kill you?'

'I do not know,' Dr Oystein murmurs. 'He was calling me a demon, but I have no idea what I could have done to enrage him.'

'I don't think it had anything to do with you,' I

sigh. 'He said something else when I was holding him, just before he died. He said . . . *Dowling*.'

Dr Oystein tenses. Zhang looks furious.

'You think Mr Dowling was behind this?' Zhang snaps.

'He must have been. Otherwise why would Mr Burke have tried to warn me about him?'

'Oystein?' Zhang asks. 'Did you hear Burke mention the clown's name?'

'No,' Dr Oystein says. 'But I am sure that B is right. That must have been what happened. Billy was our friend. He would not have tried to assassinate me out of the blue. My guess, based on what B has said, is that Mr Dowling injected Billy with some sort of drug which scrambled his senses, then programmed him to turn against me.'

'He couldn't have done that,' I frown. 'I saw him just a while ago.'

'Mr Dowling?' Dr Oystein gasps, eyes widening with fear.

'No. Mr Burke. He was with Rage and me in the East End. We left him to come back here. We stopped to play football. Then you summoned us and we came in. There can't have been time for him to be brainwashed.'

Dr Oystein rubs the area around his wound and looks thoughtful. 'That is strange. With time, a man of Mr Dowling's resources could turn any one of us, but I am not aware of a drug which could make a puppet of a man so quickly. Then again, Mr Dowling has access to chemicals that most people know nothing about. Perhaps it is something he developed himself. Either way, this is a worrying development, something new that we have to be wary of. I will investigate it further, flush out Billy's system, try to unlock the mysteries of the drug from whatever traces it has left behind.

'At least he went down fighting,' Dr Oystein says, squeezing my arm to show his support. 'Whatever Mr Dowling did to his mind, it wasn't enough to break him completely. By warning you at the end, he has done us a great service. We might have thought him a traitor otherwise. This way we know that he was simply a victim.'

'Only a coward uses a man's friends to try to destroy him,' Zhang grunts. 'If Dowling had any honour, he would never have resorted to such an underhand tactic.'

Dr Oystein smiles bitterly. 'Nobody ever accused Mr Dowling of being honourable.'

'I want to kill him,' I growl. 'I want to run him down and rip his grinning head from his body.'

'We do not know where he is,' Dr Oystein says.

'We could find him.'

The doc shakes his head. 'That is what he wants, to lure us on to his turf, to hit us when we are disoriented and not thinking clearly. He would have known the odds were stacked against Billy. If he had seriously wanted to kill me, he would have devised a more cunning plan. This was nothing more than a provocative gesture designed to stir us up, perhaps a spur-of-the-moment whim when he found Billy alone and unprotected. We must not grant him the satisfaction of a reaction.'

'So we'll do nothing?' I yell.

'We will remember,' Dr Oystein says calmly. 'And

when the day comes for us to move against Mr Dowling, we will do so in Billy Burke's name, as well as in the name of so many others who have been killed or tormented by that accursed clown.'

I stare at Dr Oystein helplessly. I don't want to wait. I want to make Mr Dowling pay immediately. But I know the doc is right. Patience isn't something that comes naturally to me, but I've been working on it and I'm learning to tell when it's time to rush into action and when it's time to hold back.

'I want to help set up the room for Mr Burke,' I mutter.

'Of course,' Dr Oystein says. 'We will see to it tonight.'

'I will organise another escort for Emma and Declan in the meantime,' Master Zhang says.

'What are you talking about?' I snap.

'I do not think that you will want to go on a mission given what has happened,' Zhang says, 'and I will not send the rest of your group without you, even assuming that they wish to proceed with it.'

'You think I'd rather sit here and brood?' I shake

my head. 'That's not me. I can't think of anything better at a time like this than keeping busy.'

Zhang's eyes narrow. 'I will not send you out if you are an emotional wreck.'

I grin like a tiger. 'I've seen lots of friends die. Burke's death won't put me off my stride. If the others are game, count me in.'

Zhang studies me for a moment, then nods. 'I have taught you well.'

'Don't give yourself all the credit,' I tell him, standing and pointing to the hole in the left side of my chest. 'I was a heartless bitch long before I came here.'

Dr Oystein and Master Zhang smile sympathetically, then take me to organise a room for Burke, where we can store and feed his reanimated corpse. In theory we're setting him up here so that we can assist him if he revitalises and becomes a thinking zombie like us. But realistically, as Zhang reminded me, there's little chance of that. It's far more likely that the room will serve as a cell for him until we give up the ghost and either set him free or put him down like a rabid dog.

EIGHT

My room-mates are solemn when I return. They try to comfort me, but it's awkward because I don't really want to talk about it. In the end I sit by the window and stare out into the darkness while they discuss the upcoming mission.

I spend a long time thinking about Burke, school, my family and friends, the old days. So much has changed. So many have been lost. It's not fair that they're all gone and I'm still here. But nobody ever said life was fair. You get what comes your way, not what you deserve.

Eventually I swim out of my daze and tune into the conversation. There's no hesitancy in the air—everyone is in, as I figured they would be. They're trying to predict what will happen on the mission, talking about all the things we'll do and see, the fights we'll win, the obstacles we'll overcome. Shane is saying he hopes we run into Mr Dowling, so that he can personally bring down the clown.

'You'd run a mile if you saw Mr Dowling in the flesh,' I snort.

'That guy doesn't bother me,' Shane says. 'I was never afraid of clowns. Mime artists on the other hand . . .'

The others laugh and start discussing the creepiness of clowns versus mime artists and a whole host of other people in costumes. Jakob says he's scared of nurses and doctors, but after all the time he spent in hospital being treated for cancer, I guess he has every right to be.

I leave my position by the window and join in and the night flies by nicely.

Just before dawn, we prepare for the trip ahead. I pour drops into my eyes to keep them moist, and make sure I have a few spare bottles in the rucksack which I'll be taking.

I sharpen my fingerbones and toe bones. Ashtat decorates hers as if they were nails, but that's too girly for me. I also file down my teeth, but not as much as normal, keeping them on the sharp side in case I have to bite my way out of a sticky situation.

None of us packs a weapon. Dr Oystein thinks weapons should be consigned to the history books. He's hoping, if we can find a way to eliminate the zombies and restore power to the living, that we can put the errors of the past behind us. Most of us would rather pack a hammer or axe, but we can see where he's coming from. We're not forbidden from using weapons in the field if the need arises, but we try to do without. Besides, with our fingerbones and fangs, who needs anything else?

I pull on fresh jeans, a tight jumper with a section cut out to expose the hole in my chest, a leather jacket and a pair of cool-looking shades. They're prescription sunglasses. We all have a few pairs. On Dr Oystein's orders, the twins have recently started to test every

Angel's eyes and track down suitable glasses. They don't restore our sight to what it was like when we were living, but they help. Contact lenses would be better, but they don't suit our dry eyes.

As I'm sticking my trusty Australian hat in my rucksack, Rage pops up in front of me and says, 'What do you think?' He's smeared green and brown paint across his face.

'We're going into suburbia,' I say, rolling my eyes, 'not the bloody jungle.'

'Over the top?'

'Big time.'

He scowls and stomps off to scrub his cheeks clean.

Ciara the dinner lady arrives with a vat of brain stew and we tuck in, downing the grey gruel, absorbing the necessary nutrients, then throwing up into buckets which Ciara sweetly passes out to us. She chats with us a bit, wishes us luck, then leaves to wash her hair and get dressed in another of her stylish outfits. Probably off to flirt with Reilly in the bowels of County Hall.

Carl spends an hour choosing his clothes for the

trip. He's even more fashion conscious than Ciara, or any girl I ever knew. He tries on at least a dozen different outfits.

'Enough,' I snap as he's studying himself in a full-length mirror for the fiftieth time. 'You're beautiful. The coolest cat in town.'

'I've got to look my best,' he says. 'Mother would spin in her grave if I got killed and didn't leave an immaculate corpse behind.'

Shane is less bothered. He doesn't even change out of the tracksuit that he was wearing earlier, though he swaps his gold chain for another in his collection, then pauses and decides to wear both. I picture him laying into scores of zombies with the chains, swinging them like nunchucks—death by bling!

'What are you laughing at?' Shane asks, catching me chuckling softly.

'An old joke,' I lie, then cast an eye over Ashtat and Jakob. They're in their usual garb, a blue robe for her, baggy clothes for him.

'Don't you think trousers would be more practical?' I ask Ashtat.

'No. I have always trained in these. I am accustomed to them.'

When we're ready, we head down to present ourselves to Dr Oystein. Emma and Declan are with him, but Master Zhang is nowhere to be seen. I note that Dr Oystein is wearing a fresh shirt, but he doesn't seem to have bandaged the wound beneath it.

'Will you hop into a Groove Tube to clear up your injury?' I ask as we spread out before him.

'No,' he says. 'Zhang dug out the bullet and the wound is only a minor nuisance.'

'It must be painful,' I note.

He shrugs. 'The pain reminds me that I must never take our safety here for granted, that we must always be aware that an attack can come at any moment, from any quarter.' He looks around at the others. 'You have all decided to go on the mission?' he asks, even though our clothes and rucksacks obviously signify that we're up for it.

A chorus of 'Yes' and 'Yeah' and 'Yup'.

'One day an Angel will turn me down,' he

mutters. 'I am almost looking forward to the shock of the rejection.'

We laugh softly, then Dr Oystein puts his hands together and bows. 'Your courage fills me with pride, and I do not say that lightly. I am privileged to have you for my charges.'

'Stop it,' Rage grunts. 'You'll make me blubber like a baby.'

'Never, Michael,' Dr Oystein says. 'I doubt if you cried even when you came out of the womb.'

'Now there's a horrible image,' I cackle.

'Less of it,' Rage growls.

'You all know what to do and how to protect Declan and Emma,' Dr Oystein goes on. 'So I will not bore you with a ponderous parting speech. But I will offer to lead you in prayer if anyone wishes to ask their god for a blessing before you depart. It is not compulsory and I will not be offended if you abstain.'

Ashtat, Shane, Carl and Jakob shuffle forward without a word. Rage takes a big step back. He looks at me, curious to see what I'll do. A few months ago I'd have joined him or stood aside on my own. But times have changed. That baby in Timothy's gallery turned my world on its head. I don't know exactly what I believe any more, except I'm convinced that there's *some* sort of higher power at work out there, otherwise how could I have dreamt of the babies in advance for all those years?

I join the others and we stand around Dr Oystein in a semi-circle as he says a short prayer. The words are his own, designed not to be exclusive. The doc never tries to force his beliefs on the rest of us. He's often said that there's room in this world for any number of gods.

At the end of his prayer he asks for a few moments of silence, so that each of us can communicate silently with our supreme being of choice. I try to think of something that isn't corny or insincere. Finally I sigh and say inside my head, *For the sake of Declan and Emma, and to atone for all those I have failed before, let me stand true.*

Then prayer time is over. Dr Oystein escorts us to the exit, issues us with a set of directions, wishes us luck and waves us off. We head down the road on our first real mission. Look out, world, here I come!

NINE

Hammersmith isn't that far from County Hall. At zombie speed, jogging, we could be there in less than an hour if we pushed ourselves. Even at human pace, allowing for a young child, it shouldn't take more than a couple of hours.

But we have to go slow. The undead hate the sunlight. It burns their skin and sears their eyes. Revitaliseds can protect themselves, dress in heavy clothes, wear sunglasses and hats. Reviveds aren't smart enough to figure that out. But they can smell the same way we can. If they get a whiff of living flesh, it might be enough to tempt them out.

Emma and Declan sprayed themselves with the strongest perfume the twins could find for them before we left our sanctuary, and that should mask their scent. But it only takes one sharp-nosed zombie latching on to their smell to bring the hordes crashing down upon us.

We cross Westminster Bridge, Emma and Declan in the middle, the rest of us fanned out around them. We've trained with humans before – Reilly normally fills in as our guinea pig – so we know what we're doing.

Even so, this feels different. With Reilly we never ventured far from the safety of County Hall. And he's a trained soldier who could defend himself if he had to. This is real, not an exercise. If we make a mistake, Emma and Declan will die.

There's none of the joking that there usually is. We're all alert, taking this seriously, saying nothing, senses trained on the area around us, ready to react to the slightest hint of an attack.

We slip by Westminster Station. There are scores of zombies down there, but luck is on our side and there aren't any resting near the entrance. We pass like ghosts, unchallenged.

Ignoring the Houses of Parliament, we cross the Square and head down the road to St James's Park. We haven't gone very far when luck deserts us. Figures spill out of one of the buildings to our left. Five zombies rush us, sights fixed on the pair of humans in our midst.

Ashtat and I protect Emma and Declan while the boys deal with the zombies. It's short and sharp. We've spent months fine-tuning our skills. On top of that we've fed regularly, we haven't had to trawl the streets for dried-up scraps of brain, so we're at our physical and mental best.

Rage and Shane each take out a couple of zombies, shattering their skulls with carefully placed blows. Carl dispatches the fifth, calmly bashing the guy's head against the pavement to crush his brain. I wince at the thuds and spray of splintered bone and blood. I know these people are already dead, that we're doing them a favour by putting them out of action. But it never feels right.

A lone female zombie darts from the shadows of a building on our right. Ashtat deals with her, whirling gracefully to deliver a kick to the undead woman's head that Bruce Lee would have been proud of. The woman's skull must have been damaged prior to this, because her head explodes like a rotten pumpkin.

'Gross,' Ashtat squeals, trying to shake goo from her foot.

'I don't like this,' Emma moans, clutching Declan tightly, looking around fearfully. I can tell that she's thinking of running.

'It's OK,' I calm her. 'You're safe with us. We know what we're doing.'

'But we're attracting attention,' she whines as another three zombies stream out of the building that the female came from.

'Not for long,' I promise, although I can't guarantee that. We could come under attack every step of the way to Hammersmith.

Jakob is fast. He races ahead of the others to tackle the new threat. Carl isn't far behind—he leaps through the air like a giant grasshopper and lands among the trio. 'Come to Daddy,' he chuckles grimly, laying into the unsuspecting zombies. The

living dead never fight among themselves. It confuses them when we turn on our own. If they could think, they'd consider us traitors to the cause.

Ashtat and I push on with Emma and Declan. Rage and Shane slot into place around us.

'The Cabinet War Rooms are just up there,' Rage says cheerfully, nodding as we come to a corner. 'Churchill had his bunker there in the Second World War. Fancy checking them out?'

'I don't think this is the time for sightseeing,' I snarl as a look of panic shoots across Emma's face. 'He's only joking,' I tell her.

'Yeah,' Rage says. 'Don't worry, love. I have a warped sense of humour.'

We make St James's Park and head for the lake, where we pause and wait for the others to catch up. This place used to teem with wildlife, exotic birds and tourist-friendly squirrels, but nothing larger than an insect moves in the park today. Zombies prefer human brains, but they can feast on animals too. The only creatures still roaming the city are those whose brains are too small to be of any interest to the undead, or those who are cunning enough to have learnt to lie low and hide.

Carl and Jakob catch up. Carl is grinning, wiping blood from his hands with clumps of grass. Jakob looks as serious as ever.

Emma is panting hard. 'I don't think this was a good idea. Maybe we should go back.'

'It will be fine,' Ashtat assures her.

'We don't have to worry so much in the parks,' I tell her. 'Reviveds mostly stick to the shadows in the daytime. They avoid open spaces like this.'

'What about when we get back on to the streets again?' she says.

I shrug. 'There are zombies everywhere. But you knew that before we set out. It's a risk, but not the biggest gamble in the world. You stand a better chance with us than you would on your own.'

'But if we returned to County Hall . . .' Emma wavers.

'We can if you want,' Rage sniffs. 'But then you're stuck with us for the rest of your days. What do you think, Declan? Do you want to come home with your undead Uncle Rage?'

Declan says nothing, but turns his face away and buries it in his mother's skirt.

'If you want to retreat, tell us and we'll take you,' Carl says patiently. 'But if you're going to change your mind, now's the time. We can slip back without any hassle. Nobody can predict how many of the buggers might be lying in wait for us further on.'

Emma hesitates, torn between hope and fear. Nobody says anything. It's not our job to persuade her one way or the other, merely to help her however we can.

'OK,' she finally croaks. 'We'll go on.'

'Great,' Shane beams. 'You know it makes sense.'

We advance, holding our formation around the shivering humans. As I said to Emma, it should be safe in the park, but we don't take chances. A zombie could have carved a niche for itself in one of the trees, or dug a hole in the soil and be lying covered by twigs and leaves, or be resting at the bottom of the shallow lake with its mouth closed and its nose pinched shut. We stay alert, taking nothing for granted, each one of us all too aware that in this world of the living dead a single mistake can be the end of you.

TEN

We hike through St James's Park, skirt Buckingham Palace and enter Green Park. That links up with Hyde Park, and soon we're strolling along as if on a fun day out. We stick to the middle of the park, so we have a clear view in all directions.

We relax our guard slightly and Emma lets Declan run around, chasing after him, playing games. But we don't let either of them slip too far away, wary of hidden threats.

The grass has grown wild since the downfall of mankind. Old scraps of rubbish blow across it.

Weeds snake through the bones of human carcasses. But this is still a soothing place. In these green stretches it's possible to imagine that the apocalypse never happened. If I use my imagination, it could be a quiet Sunday morning, early, before any joggers or tourists are about. I might be on my way home from an all-night party, Mum and Dad waiting for me, angry but concerned, school on Monday, boring but reassuring, all my friends to catch up with.

I shake my head and frown. There's no use thinking that way. The world's gone to hell and the only way to deal with it is to accept it for what it is. No point trying to live in the past. That's for saps.

We eventually run out of park and pause to prepare for the next stretch. It's a fairly straight, wide road most of the way to Hammersmith. On paper it's a doddle. In the flesh it looks a lot less straightforward.

'What about a car?' Emma asks, spotting one stranded in the road nearby.

'The noise would draw attention,' Carl tells her.

'But we could move faster than the zombies, couldn't we?' she persists.

'Yes,' Carl says, 'but they could attack from the side or throw themselves in the way and make us crash. Then we'd be trapped and they'd just have to swarm round the car and force their way in.'

'It will be fine,' Ashtat reassures Emma. 'You survived on the streets for months, and that was without our help.'

'But I didn't move about this much,' Emma says. 'I only travelled short distances any time I left my base. And I kept to the shadows. We'll be in full view of any watching zombies out here.'

'That's the best place to be,' I chuckle, pointing at the hole in my chest. 'When they see this, and some of our other wounds, they'll know we're undead. Seeing us in the mix, they'll assume we're all zombies. I mean, everyone knows that zombies and the living don't get along, right?'

Emma licks her lips nervously. 'If you're sure . . .'

'We are,' Rage grunts and we move out of the park and on to the road.

Things go more smoothly than we anticipated. We're attacked several times, but by individuals or small groups. And they only cause us any difficulties if they're hiding behind cars and leap out at us suddenly as we approach. The rest – the ones lounging in buildings on either side of the road – are easy to deal with, as we see them coming from a long way off and have plenty of time to get ready for them.

'This is too easy,' Shane mutters as he rips another zombie's brain from its skull then wipes his hand clean on the back of the dead creature's shirt.

'Don't get cocky,' I snap.

'I'm not,' he says. 'I'm worried. When you have things this easy, it usually means you're going to run into all kinds of trouble later.'

'Don't be a pessimist,' Carl grunts, but I know he's thinking the same thing. We all are, except maybe Rage. He's the sort of guy who always expects a smooth ride, since he figures the world was made for him in the first place.

But despite our fears the big catastrophe fails to

materialise. We aren't attacked by gangs. We never need to break formation or run. We don't end up trapped in a building with no way out.

In a weird way it's an anti-climax. We were ready for fireworks, but we barely have to bloody our fists. Still, I guess that's a good thing, if not for us, then definitely for Emma and Declan.

We run into a minor problem in Hammersmith. There's a flyover we want to pass under, but the shaded area is packed with zombies. A few catch sight of us and get to their feet. For a second it looks like we're in trouble. But then they spot the hole in my chest and the green moss growing from the cuts on some of the others. The zombies lie down again, not bothering to shuffle forward to investigate more closely, never realising that there are a couple of jokers in the pack.

We find another way around, making use of side roads, and arrive at our destination as the midday sun is burning bright in the sky. The humans are holed up in a block of offices. We pause outside the entrance and stare at the building. It still feels like we've had it too easy. I half-expect Mr Dowling and his mutants to come abseiling down.

Instead what happens is something almost as surprising, but nowhere near as alarming. Declan speaks for the first time since I've known him.

'Doggy.'

All of us gawp at the normally silent boy. Emma's face lights up and she hugs him, then starts to cry happily. Maybe she thought he would never speak again. But Declan ignores her tears. He's looking at the road behind us and he points over her shoulder.

'Doggy,' he says again.

'Bloody hell,' Shane laughs. 'He's not wrong. Look.'

We slipped under a rising entry barrier on our way into the yard surrounding the building. Now when I look back, I spot a large, hairy sheepdog standing on the other side.

'Isn't it beautiful,' Ashtat coos as I do a stunned double take. She drops to her knees and makes a clicking noise with her tongue and teeth. 'Here, doggy.'

The dog ignores her. Its tail isn't wagging. It's staring at us.

The sheepdog is white at the front, turning to grey further back. Its hair is dirty and matted with dried bloodstains. The others are enchanted by it, not having seen a live dog since before the zombies rose up and killed them all for their brains. They join Ashtat in calling and whistling, trying to get it to come closer.

I'm less excited by the dog. In fact I'm seriously disturbed. When I was making my way to Timothy's gallery after Rage had pushed me off the London Eye, I came across a dog just like this. It was resting in the road and ran off when I tried to get it to come. It had the same markings and stains as this one.

Maybe the dog followed me and has been trailing me ever since, but I doubt it. I would surely have seen it before if it had made its home close to County Hall. So what other explanations are there? Is it coincidence that our paths have crossed again? Or perhaps it's a different dog that just looks the same?

I glance around, uneasy but not sure why. As Ashtat and the rest call to the dog and click their

fingers, I suddenly shout at it, 'Get out of here, you ugly mutt!'

The dog bolts and everyone glares at me.

'What did you do that for?' Ashtat cries.

'I don't like dogs,' I lie.

'Even so, you didn't have to scare it off,' Ashtat pouts. 'I think we could have persuaded it to come to us. You could have simply stood back.'

'There was blood on its fur,' I improvise. 'It might have been zombie blood. It could have infected Emma and Declan.'

Ashtat frowns and considers that. As she's thinking it over, the door to the building opens behind us and someone calls out chirpily, 'I knew that was B Smith even before I heard your voice. I recognised the smell.'

We whirl round. The others squint at the dark-skinned stranger on the steps, not sure what to make of his unexpected greeting. But he's no stranger to me, and as he stands there smirking, I take a trembling step forward and croak his name with disbelief.

'*Vinyl?*'

ELEVEN

Vinyl was my best friend back when I was a normal girl. We'd been friends since we were toddlers. Being a racist, my dad forbade me from having anything to do with black kids. But in that one instance I disobeyed him. I pretended to blank Vinyl, but I'd see him behind Dad's back. I knew Dad would beat the crap out of me if he ever found out, but I liked Vinyl too much to drive him away.

Vinyl was brighter than the rest of us. He got upgraded to a better school when his mum made him sit a Mensa test and his potential was uncovered.

I'm sure he would have stopped hanging out with me after another month or two, and that would have been the end of our friendship. But he was still one of the gang the day before the zombie attacks, when I last spoke to him on the phone.

'What the hell are you doing here?' I ask once we're safely inside the building and the door has been locked.

'I'm your guide,' he says as if it's the most ordinary thing in the world. 'I'm here to lead you guys to New Kirkham. That's the name of the compound.'

'But how did you get here? How did you survive and end up doing a job like this?'

'I'll explain it all shortly,' Vinyl says, cool as ever. 'Come and meet the rest of the group first. We're not moving out until morning, so we have all of the afternoon and night to chat.'

He leads us through to a massive atrium, nothing over our heads except the roof high above. You can see all of the floors from here, the offices set just behind the outer corridors.

Eight humans wait in the centre of the atrium, three men, two women, a couple of teenagers and a girl about Declan's age. They look nervous. There are also a pair of Angels, Pearse and Conall, sitting slightly apart from the humans, playing cards. Rage hails the Angels and trots over to join their game.

'Pearse and Conall came with me from New Kirkham,' Vinyl says. 'Dr Oystein likes us to team up with his Angels for operations like this.'

'You know Dr Oystein?' I ask, head still spinning.

'Haven't met him. Heard lots about him from Mr Burke.'

'Burke?' If the blood could drain from my face, it would.

Before I can ask any more questions, we're welcomed by the humans we've come to escort. They're scared of us, that's clear, but do their best to hide it. They invite us to eat with them, but Ashtat explains that we don't need food.

The little girl asks Declan if he wants to play. He shakes his head and clings to his mum. Emma laughs and slots in with the other living people, telling

Declan he has nothing to be afraid of, unconsciously turning her back on us and abandoning us for those more like herself, which is understandable.

The little girl pesters Declan, urging him to play with her. Vinyl smiles and whispers to me, 'That's Liz. She's an orphan and hasn't had any other children to play with for as long as she's been with the group. I don't think she'll take no for an answer.'

As Liz keeps plugging away at a scared-looking Declan, some of the survivors take us on a tour of the building and tell us how they holed up here not long after the zombies attacked. They took on the undead with knives, heavy office equipment and crudely fashioned spears, fighting them for the right to call this place home.

Once they've shown us around, they leave us in the atrium and go to celebrate their final night here and ready themselves for the journey. I gather that a few of them would rather stay, but they voted and the majority were in favour of heading for pastures less confining.

Ashtat, Carl, Shane and Jakob join Rage and the

other Angels. Vinyl and I slip away by ourselves and wind up in the canteen.

'It's been a long time,' Vinyl notes softly, taking a chair and opening a bottle of orange juice.

'Looks like it's been longer for you than me,' I grunt. I haven't aged since my heart was ripped from my chest, but Vinyl looks about five years older. Life has taken its toll on him.

'You look pretty much the way I remember you,' Vinyl says. 'Except for the obvious differences.'

'I don't know what you're talking about,' I say sweetly, smoothing back the wisps of moss which surround the hole where my heart used to be.

'That's got to hurt, hasn't it?' he asks.

'Not as much as you'd think. We don't feel pain the same way that we did when we were alive. It stings all the time, but I'm not in agony.'

Vinyl stares at me sadly.

'Stuff your sympathy where the sun don't shine,' I snap. 'I don't need it and I sure as hell don't want it.'

'Death hasn't mellowed you,' Vinyl laughs.

'Damn straight,' I huff. 'I'm grumpier than ever,

and I have fangs now, so don't get on the wrong side of me.'

Vinyl shakes his head happily. 'I've missed you, B.'

'I've missed you too,' I mutter, then lean forward, but not too close, wary as I always am around the living, not wanting to accidentally infect him. 'Any idea what happened to my mum and dad?'

Vinyl sighs. 'No. I haven't seen them. Sorry.'

'Did your parents get out?'

'No,' he whispers and his jaw trembles slightly.

'What about the old gang, Stagger Lee, Trev, Meths. Any of them make it?'

'None that I know of.' He shrugs. 'But there are lots of compounds. People got scattered all over the place. How about you? Do you know anyone who survived?'

'Only Mr Burke. And maybe Mrs Reed, kind of.'

I tell Vinyl about that last day in school, listing our friends who perished, at least those I can remember—I think I've forgotten one or two names, strange as that seems. I also tell him about the teachers who were killed, the students who got away with my dad, and how Mrs Reed became some sort of brain-eating cross between a zombie and a human.

'You're pulling my leg,' he snorts.

'I'm not.'

He scratches his head. 'But if she wasn't a proper zombie, what was she then?'

'I don't know. I haven't thought about her in ages. I remember clocking it at the time, thinking it was weird, but too much has happened since for me to follow it up. Not that I could, even if I wanted to. I don't know what happened to her, if she got out, where she might be.'

'Maybe she's still in our old school. She could be teaching zombies these days. *B is for Brains,*' he says, mimicking her voice.

'Don't be an arse,' I grin, but my smile fades as I tell him about Tyler Bayor and how I let my dad turn me into something even lower than a slug.

Vinyl is grim-faced when I finish. He looks at me harshly. 'Tyler was solid,' he says gruffly.

'I know,' I croak.

'He didn't deserve that.'

'No.'

'I warned you about what would happen, didn't I? I said you had to stand up to your dad, that you'd turn out as bad as him if you didn't.'

'I don't think you ever put it quite like that,' I growl.

'I came pretty damn close,' he says. 'The only thing that stopped me being that blunt was that I knew how angry you got when anyone said anything bad about your father.'

'Yeah, well, that was before I saw him in all his glory. I'm not standing up for him now, am I?'

Vinyl frowns. 'You really ran back into the school instead of leaving with him and going your own way later?'

'Yeah.'

'That was dumb, wasn't it?'

I laugh and stretch out my right hand to knock knuckles. Then I remember that I'm a zombie who can't touch him, and settle for a cheesy thumbs up.

TWELVE

I tell Vinyl about my life since I was killed. The bit he enjoys most is when I describe climbing the London Eye.

'You really scaled it using just your hands?'

'Yeah.'

'Wicked.'

When I'm done, it's Vinyl's turn. He was at his new school the day of the attacks. By luck he was outside for a phys-ed class when the world went haywire. He fled with some of his classmates, then headed home. He couldn't find his mum and dad.

'So maybe they're alive, in another compound,' I suggest.

'Nah,' he says sadly. 'I met a neighbour of ours a few months later. He saw them get killed. He said both were properly slaughtered, their brains ripped out, so at least I don't have to worry about them stumbling around in a monstrous state.'

Vinyl survived that first night by locking himself into a bank vault.

'You what?' I hoot.

'I figured a bank would be as safe a place as any,' he grins. 'The vaults are operated by time locks. As long as we could keep out the zombies until the vaults were due to shut, we could slip inside and they wouldn't be able to get at us.'

'You were always oozing with brains,' I mutter.

'Yeah, baby,' he crows. 'I'd be a prize scalp for one of your crowd.'

Vinyl found refuge in one of our local banks, spent that first night locked up nice and tight – he says he slept on a bed of banknotes that must have been worth a million pounds, but I think he's making that bit up – then struck out for the countryside in the morning.

'Most of the people in the bank stayed behind,' he snorts. 'They thought the army would rescue them. I figured there wasn't a hope of that. When a city like London falls, there's no quick recovery.'

Vinyl roughed it for a few weeks in the country, avoiding contact with anyone. Then he stumbled across one of the first compounds to be set up and threw in his lot with them.

'It fell less than a week later,' he sighs. 'We underestimated the sheer bloody determination of the undead. They kept coming and coming. They wore us down, picked holes in our barriers, and next thing we knew they were swarming the place.'

He made it out with a few others and went looking for another compound. He found New Kirkham – though it didn't have a name then – and he's been there ever since, only leaving it at times like this, to guide other humans to sanctuary.

'I got closely involved in the running of the place,' he says. 'Age doesn't matter any more. Qualifications are irrelevant. It all boils down to what you know and how you operate under pressure. I'd learnt a lot of lessons from the collapse of the first compound and I was able to make suggestions to shore up our defences.'

'So you're a Big Chief now?' I grin. 'Power, a throne, a harem?'

'Yeah,' he deadpans. 'A gold-rimmed toilet, caviar for breakfast, the works.'

The army rolled by a month or so after Vinyl had arrived in New Kirkham. They wanted to put their stamp on the place, but the residents were happy with things the way they were. They rejected the offer of help and have remained one of the few truly independent mainland compounds.

'Were the soldiers pissed?' I ask.

He shrugs. 'They thought we were fools, but they left us in peace. Told us not to come crying to them when it all broke down. But so far it hasn't.'

One day, out of the blue, Billy Burke came calling. He was with a group of survivors. He'd led them out of London with the help of a few Angels. The newcomers were accepted gratefully—there's plenty of space in the compound, so the locals are happy to admit stragglers as long as they're willing to toe the line and work hard.

'Burke asked for volunteers to come back with the Angels and act as guides for future groups,' Vinyl says. 'A lot of the survivors in London don't trust the Angels. They're more likely to accept an invitation of help if someone living is involved.'

Not many people offered to become guides. Life was hard enough as it was. They faced assaults every night. They'd seen horrors in the towns and cities that they'd never forget. They were loath to return. Vinyl was one of the few who said he'd help.

'Fancied yourself as a hero?' I chuckle.

He pulls a face. 'It just seemed like the right thing to do.' I raise a mocking eyebrow and he sighs. 'OK, the truth is, I've had really bad nightmares since I escaped. The sort where I piss myself and wake up screaming and shaking. I thought I might be able to stop the bad dreams if I confronted my fears.'

My smile fades. I'm sorry now that I teased him. 'Has it helped?' I ask.

'Not really. But once I'd made a few runs with the Angels, I felt compelled to carry on. I saw how they risked their lives for people who in some cases openly despised them. Once I was part of the gang, I didn't feel like it would be fair to pull out.' Vinyl grimaces. 'Burke probably bet on that. He's a clever sod. Not much gets by him. I'm sure he knew that once he'd got me to do one run, I wouldn't be able to . . .'

Vinyl catches my expression and trails off into silence. 'What's wrong?' he asks quietly, although he can probably guess.

I tell him about Burke, how Mr Dowling must have messed with his mind and sent him to kill Dr Oystein, the way I scratched him while I was disarming him, holding him in my arms while he died. I can't cry, but my voice shakes and I moan during the telling.

Vinyl stares at the ceiling glumly when I'm finished. 'That sucks. Burke always said he'd be taken down sooner rather than later, that you couldn't throw in your lot with the undead and expect to last

110

very long. That didn't bother him. But to be turned by one of your own, on your home turf . . .'

'I had to do it,' I snap. 'He was shooting at Dr Oystein. He had to be stopped. I didn't want to kill him. It was an accident. But he left me no choice.'

'Easy,' Vinyl soothes me. 'I wasn't having a go. I just mean it's a pity that he couldn't have been killed by zombies, out in the field, fighting to help a group of people to freedom. He deserved a hell of an end, not to go meekly.'

'Yeah, well, few of us get what we deserve,' I sniff.

'Tell me about it,' Vinyl sighs.

We're silent for a while. I think about telling Vinyl that Burke was vaccinated, that we're keeping him locked up in case he ever recovers, but I'm not sure how he'd take that. Remembering what he said about his parents, I figure he might be of the opinion that it would be better to execute our old teacher. I don't want to argue with him, so it's easier to say nothing about it.

'Does it change anything, Burke being dead?' I finally ask.

'Nah,' Vinyl says. 'I never saw much of him anyway. I'll carry on the same as usual. But I'll miss him. He was a star.'

'Yeah,' I mumble. I know I shouldn't feel horrible or guilty, but I do.

'You couldn't help it, B,' Vinyl says softly, seeing the self-hatred in my eyes.

'I know.'

'But you feel bad anyway?'

I nod stiffly.

'Best way to make up for it is to do what Burke would have wanted,' Vinyl says. 'See this lot to safety. Then return and rescue some more of the living.'

'Yeah. But how many more good deeds do I have to do before I stop feeling like a rat?' I ask.

Vinyl shrugs. 'If I knew that, I'd be a very wise man. But I'm just a guy who likes old records and hanging out with racist birds.'

'Less of it,' I growl as he stands and yawns, but I'm grinning.

We return to the atrium and spend the rest of the evening and early part of the night with the other

Angels. Pearse and Conall have done this run a few times and they've become good friends with Vinyl. He gets to know the rest of the gang and amuses them with some stories about me from the distant past. We play cards – all of us careful never to pass cards directly to Vinyl or come within scraping distance of him – and Vinyl downs a couple of beers.

Emma comes to see us later, carrying a tray of sandwiches. She tries to make small talk. I think she feels bad for having deserted us. Vinyl munches a few of the sandwiches, chats with Emma, makes her laugh. She leaves looking less solemn.

'You're a real man of the people, aren't you?' I smirk.

'A Big Chief has to be,' he winks. 'I plan on running for prime minister when we get this world back in order. I might need her vote.'

'You really think we can knock the world back into shape?' I ask sceptically.

'With people like you and me on the case, how can we fail?' he laughs.

Eventually Vinyl bids us goodnight. 'I know you

guys don't need any shut-eye, but this boy soldier needs his beauty sleep.'

'Will you bed down with the others?' I ask.

'No, I'll be sleeping by myself, the way I always do.'

'Because nobody wants to share a bed with you?' I joke.

Vinyl winces. 'No. Because I don't want to scare anyone when I wake up screaming.'

With a short wave he heads for bed, leaving the darkest, most twisted hours of the night to those of us best suited to them.

THIRTEEN

In the morning we ready the humans and make sure they've sprayed perfume or aftershave all over. They wear old, dusty clothes, and have stained the fronts of many of them with their own blood, which they've extracted with syringes over the last few days, to make it look as if they've fed from the living. We warn them not to talk when we're outside, unless it's essential. No yawning, burping or farting. They're not to look around or show interest in anything.

We need them to appear as corpse-like as possible. Their disguise won't hold if any zombies come close, but from a distance they shouldn't draw too much attention. Of course every member of the undead will be interested in anything that braves the sunlight world, but we won't be the only zombies out there on the streets. I've seen groups at large before, packs which had to move on when their shelter burnt down, or stragglers who fell behind when they were chasing prey and who weren't prepared to admit defeat.

It won't be easy getting these guys to New Kirkham, but it's not Mission Impossible either. A slice of luck will be welcome, but we can probably do without it if we have to.

When everyone's good to go, we let ourselves out, cross the river and head south. Pearse and Conall lead the way. They're an odd couple. Both have ginger hair, but there the similarities end. Pearse is small and skinny, whereas Conall is built like a tower of bricks, almost a match for Rage.

They wear distinctive headgear. Conall prefers a pair of baseball caps, one the right way round, the other back to front to cover his neck. But Pearse has opted for a beekeeper's hat, mesh and all. He says it's because he has naturally delicate skin. 'The sun burnt the hell out of me even when I was alive,' he laughs. 'I have to be extra cautious now.'

Vinyl moves among the humans, circling constantly, quietly reassuring them, communicating any commands that we wish to pass on, holding everyone together.

I'm almost as nervous as the living. I don't know this area. I was an East End girl—nowhere east of Wapping fazed me in the slightest. I've adapted to Central London since moving to County Hall and have started to feel comfortable there. But places like Putney and Roehampton are alien to me.

We stick to open areas as much as we can, the middle of wide roads, parks when we come to them. I thought suburbia would be a breeze after the narrow streets of the city, but we're attacked far more frequently than we were on our way from Westminster to Hammersmith.

Fortunately there are rarely more than three or four zombies per group. They tend to gather in small packs here, making their base in what used to be family homes, rather than pile into a factory or warehouse in their dozens. Vinyl laughs quietly when I mention that.

'It must be a middle-class thing,' he says. 'The posh lot crave privacy, even in death. Don't want to be mixing with the wrong sort of people.'

We have a good chuckle, but Vinyl is serious when I comment on the frequency of the attacks.

'They're hungrier than the zombies in the more central areas,' he says. 'Not so many people out here, therefore not so many corpses. There used to be more of the undead when I first started coming this way. A lot have moved on, either heading for the city centre or off to find richer pickings in the country. Those who've remained must be desperate. They'll have a serious sniff at anything that passes, just in case.'

The attacks are more of a nuisance than a threat, though I'm sure the survivors don't see them that way. They tense every time a zombie lunges at us, follow each brief battle with wide, worried eyes.

They're sweating with fear, so they have to keep reapplying scent.

By early afternoon we're marching through the countryside proper and the humans relax slightly. It's a cloudy day, but the clouds keep breaking and letting the sun through in bursts. Nice for the humans, a pain for us. I want to put on my sunglasses, but only a few of us can wear them at a time. It would look suspicious if we all went marching around in matching shades—reviveds aren't the sharpest tools in the box, but they're not completely clueless.

We stop for lunch by a tree with plenty of shade, on a hill with a clear view of the open fields. The Angels don't eat, but the living tuck into more of Emma's sandwiches. They sit on the grass and treat this like a picnic, whispering away happily, washing down the food with water and fizzy drinks.

There are no zombies anywhere in sight, which frees us to pull out our sunglasses and put them on. The world comes into much sharper focus and my eyes stop stinging. I breathe a happy sigh and wish for the millionth time since I revitalised that my eye-lids still functioned.

The little girl, Liz, finishes eating before the adults and decides she wants to climb the tree. Shane checks it out first, scampering up the trunk like a squirrel with his extra sharp nails, to make sure there are no nasty surprises lying in store for her. When he gives her the all-clear, she clambers up and starts to play. After a while, she calls for Declan to join her, and though he resists at first, eventually he wanders across and lets Liz help pull him up.

I watch the kids playing together, and I'd be lying if I said I didn't have a nice warm feeling inside. But it's nowhere near as warm as the sun when the clouds part. With a scowl I take off my hat to scratch my scalp, then squat beside Vinyl, who's chewing a blade of grass and peering off into the distance, cool as you like. 'How much further is this place?' I ask.

'We won't get there today,' he says. 'There's a safe house we use, a few hours down the road. We'll rest there overnight, head off bright and early, should make New Kirkham before midday tomorrow.'

'Aren't there any compounds closer than that?'

He shrugs. 'A few, but they're run by the army. We don't have much to do with them.'

'You're not a fan of soldiers, are you?' I note.

'I don't mind them,' he says. 'They've done a good job in lots of places, even if they tend to govern with an iron fist. But they rule the airwaves completely and crack down on anyone who doesn't toe the line. And nobody ever found out how the zombie virus spread so swiftly in the first place. Many think it was a military experiment gone wrong, and there have been lots of rumours of places like the underground complex you were telling me about, where they're conducting all sorts of horrible tests.'

'On zombies?' I ask.

'I think so, yeah.'

'Why does that bother you?'

He shrugs. 'They were normal people once. They're the enemy now, obviously, and we have to eradicate them if we're to restore order to the world. But we should still treat them with respect. I mean, how would you like it if they were cutting up *your* mum?'

'If it helped them find a cure . . .' I mutter.

'There's no cure,' Vinyl snorts. 'They're just look-ing for a virus which will wipe out the undead, save us the job of having to shoot them all. And I'm fine with that. But according to the rumour mill, some of the scientists are slicing up the dead for sport, toying with them, tormenting them.'

I think back to my time on the *Belfast*, Dan-Dan and Lord Luca and the rest of those stinking-rich bastards. I recall the way they treated the living dead as vermin, as if we existed just to entertain them. They thought they could do anything to us, that we didn't matter.

'You know what, Vinyl?' I sniff. 'You're not bad for a human.'

He chuckles. 'That's the strangest compliment I've ever been paid.'

As the rest of the living finish their sandwiches and tidy up – old habits die hard – a small bird flutters down out of nowhere and begins picking at the crumbs. Everyone stops and smiles at our unlikely visitor. While lots of birds are still at large, they tend to give people a wide berth, since zombies will catch them if possible to eat their bite-sized brains.

'Any idea what sort of a bird it is?' I ask Vinyl softly.

'A finch, I think, but I'm not sure. Birds were never my thing.'

The bird picks up a crust and flies up into the tree, settling on a branch well above Liz and Declan, who are still happily playing. It tears into the crust, pinning it against the branch with its feet, shaking its feathers as it wriggles about.

Some specks of dirt fly from the bird's feathers as it's shaking them, and one of the specks hits Liz's forehead. She brushes it away without blinking, thinking nothing of it. But the dirt leaves a stain behind that unsettles me. Removing my sunglasses, I stare until my eyes focus, and when I see the colour of the stain, my teeth grind together with fear.

It's red.

'Declan,' I call, trying not to let my anxiety show, praying that I'm working myself up into a panic over nothing. The boy looks down at me. 'Come here.'

Declan frowns then ignores me.

'Emma.' She glances at me, still smiling about the bird. 'Call him to you. Now.'

Emma notes my tense expression. She doesn't know what I'm worried about, but she reacts immediately. 'Declan. Come to me.'

'Play,' he says stubbornly. He was the most obedient boy I've ever seen up until this, but now that Liz has lured him out of his shell, he's become more like other children his age.

'What's wrong?' Vinyl asks, as others start to pay attention.

'The bird,' I explain. 'There was blood on its feathers. A drop hit Liz. It might be blood from an animal or a corpse, but it could also be from –'

Liz screams before I can finish. It's a very specific type of scream, one I've heard lots of times before, one I had hoped never to hear again.

'Jump, Declan!' I roar, turning to Vinyl and Emma. 'Catch him,' I bark as I run to the tree and climb the trunk.

Vinyl and Emma realise what is happening and

they start shouting at Declan to jump, holding out their arms, promising to catch him. But the boy has frozen. He stares at the people on the ground – others are shouting at him too now – then at Liz, who is shuddering and frothing, shaking as she clings to the tree, eyes rolling madly in their sockets.

Scared by all the activity, the bird abandons the crust of bread and flies away, but the damage has already been done, and I curse the innocent creature as it takes to the sky and swiftly disappears from sight.

Reaching the two children, I wrap my arms round Liz and hold her as still as I can. Declan is looking at me with wide eyes. His cheeks are pale and he's trembling.

'Go,' I tell him.

Declan shakes his head and whispers, 'Liz?'

'Go!' I shout and bare my fangs to shock him into action. The tactic works and Declan hurls himself from the tree with a frightened shriek. Vinyl and Emma catch him between them, then Emma buries his face in her chest and rushes away with him as the other humans and Angels press closer to the tree. Many of the people are crying.

'Liz,' a woman moans, but nobody else says her name or pleads with me to stop. They know what has happened and they know what has to be done.

As Liz shudders and undergoes the change from a living girl to an undead monstrosity, I quickly check her legs and arms for any evidence of a c-shaped scar. If she has been vaccinated by Dr Oystein's team, one of us can escort her back to County Hall, in case she revitalises later.

But there's no scar. The girl is without hope. If I let this run its natural course, she will become a brain-dead revived, with no chance of ever regaining her senses.

'Get everyone away from here,' I tell Vinyl. 'They don't need to see this. And I don't want any of them to get splattered by her blood.'

'Come on,' Vinyl says, and quickly shepherds the survivors away. The Angels remain, grim-faced but supportive.

'Do you want me to do it?' Rage asks. 'I know you're sensitive when children are involved.'

'There's no room for sensitivity in this world,' I say sadly.

And then, before Liz has completed her awful evolution, before bones force their way out through her fingertips and her teeth lengthen into fangs, I press her skull against the tree trunk, make a fist, and release the unfortunate orphan from the horror.

FOURTEEN

We bury Liz in a deep grave and the humans say some prayers over it. I don't hang around to listen. I spend the time wiping my hands through the grass, over and over, cleaning them of every last horrible stain. The others leave me be. Each one of them knows what this is like. We've all executed a zombie like Liz before, some of them even younger than she was. There's nothing you can say at a time like this. Liz was a doomed killer, but she was also a little girl, and while I know I had to do what I did, I still feel absolutely wretched, and will for a long time to come.

We press on once the living are done praying. We march in solemn silence, the survivors glancing at us bitterly every so often. I know what they're thinking—*If we'd stayed in Hammersmith, Liz would be alive now.* And they're right. That's what makes it so hard to bear. We're trying to do good here, but a little girl is dead because of our interference. There's no getting away from that.

We reach the safe house and settle down for the night, the humans in a few of the rooms, the Angels in another. I sit in a corner by myself, lost in thought. Vinyl enters at one point, to try and comfort me, but I just shake my head at him and he leaves without saying anything.

In the morning, while the living are having a quick breakfast, Ashtat approaches me. 'Will you be OK?' she asks.

'As much as I can be,' I sigh.

'We can send you back to County Hall if you prefer.'

'No, I'd rather stick with the mission. It'll be easier not to think about it if I can keep busy.'

She nods. 'As you wish.' She hesitates, then decides to press on. 'You were the only one who saw the blood strike her. If you had not reacted as fast as you did, she might have infected Declan before we could get to them.'

'I know. But still . . .'

'Yes,' Ashtat says. 'Still . . .'

She offers me a brief, weary smile, then goes to check on the humans. I spend a few more minutes thinking about Liz, then put the morbid thoughts behind me and crack on with the job at hand. There's never much time for reflection these days. You roll with the punches or you fall to the ground and weep until the flesh drops from your bones. There's no place in between.

The sleep has done the living good, and although the loss of Liz has scarred them, they do their best to soldier on as if nothing has happened. They're excited about the prospect of finding safe haven in New Kirkham, and we have to keep reminding them not to talk to one another. They want to discuss their new home and what life will be like once they've settled in, if they'll find any friends or family members among the townsfolk. We're only concerned with getting them there alive and well. We don't believe in looking too far ahead.

Finally, shortly before midday, we crest a hill and spot New Kirkham. It's a converted town. The people who decided to turn it into a base built several tall, steel-plated walls round the perimeter, topped with spikes and barbed wire. There are small platforms situated along the walls at regular intervals, manned by guards with guns, flame-throwers and whatever other weapons they've managed to scavenge.

Thousands of zombies mill around the compound. They scratch at the walls, snarl at the guards, leap at the spikes.

The humans among us gasp at the sight of the beleaguered town. A couple cross themselves.

'Why the hell have you brought us here?' one of the men growls angrily.

'It's not as bad as it looks,' Vinyl says.

'You're kidding me,' the man retorts. 'That's a disaster waiting to happen. You think we're going to lock ourselves into a death trap like that? We were a million times better off where we were. Take us back to London.'

'We can if you want,' Vinyl shrugs. 'We're not gonna force you to stay. But I suggest you enter with us and have a look round before you decide. This is one of the safest places in the country. We've studied the zombies. We know their strengths and limits, and built the walls to those specifications. They can't punch through. They can't leap over or climb them. They can't dig under them. We keep watch on the living dead every minute of the day and night, from every angle. I'm not saying our barriers are impenetrable – only a fool makes those sorts of boasts – but in all my months here, not a single zombie has breached our defences.'

'But if they did break through?' Emma asks, clutching Declan close—he's retreated into his customary silent shell since the incident with Liz yesterday, and I think it will be a long time before he comes out of it again.

'There are escape tunnels,' Vinyl says. 'Nine already dug, six more under construction. They run for hundreds of metres deep underground and open up far from the sight of any nearby zombies.

'We grow our own crops,' Vinyl continues, pointing to tilled plots within the walls. 'There are two wells. We also grow crops elsewhere and transport them in through the tunnels, along with other supplies which we forage for. But if the worst came to pass, and we got penned in, we could survive on what we harvest inside.'

'What I don't understand,' Carl mutters, 'is why your guards aren't picking off targets. There are thousands of zombies lined up outside the walls. Why don't you shoot them all?'

'Other survivors made that mistake,' Vinyl says grimly. 'We did too, at the compound we established before New Kirkham. It seemed so easy—the zombies came in their masses, we picked them off with ease, we thought we could keep going indefinitely. We planned to rid England of tens of thousands of zombies all by ourselves.

'The first problem we encountered made us wary, but wasn't enough to merit a change of plan. Lots of corpses create mounds. Other zombies can use those as springboards to leap the walls. You'd have to build a wall several storeys high to stop them getting over, or else go out regularly in some sort of armoured bulldozer to clear the stacks of corpses.

'We might have explored those possibilities in greater detail, but then we hit the second problem and that was the real killer—the insects. No wall in the world can be built high enough to keep those buggers out.'

'What are you talking about?' I frown.

'Insects aren't especially attracted to mobile zombies,' he explains. 'They don't draw much distinction between the living and the undead. But if I fired a bullet through your head . . .' he cocks a finger and pretends to shoot me '. . . your corpse would start to break down. Flies, maggots and other creepy-crawlies would rush to gorge themselves on your gooey remains. Rats and mice would burrow through your flesh. Birds and bats would pick at you. All sorts of creatures would feast on you until they'd nibbled you down to the bone, however long that might take.

'The thing we fear more than anything else is infection,' Vinyl says quietly. 'Like we saw yesterday, with Liz. We can deal with direct assaults. But insects, rodents and birds can spread the undead disease too. A fly could be eating its fill on a zombie corpse. Some blood sticks to its legs. It buzzes over the wall into New Kirkham, looking for fresh pickings. Settles on someone's lips while they're asleep. The blood rubs off. The person transforms. Trouble in paradise.

'Now a single fly and a lone zombie on the loose aren't that big a deal. Again, yesterday's tragedy with Liz shows that we can limit the damage when it's an isolated incident. But millions of flies, feasting on thousands of zombie corpses, drifting our way on a nice cool breeze . . . That would be the end of life as we know it.'

'So you don't dare kill the zombies?' I ask.

'Not loads of them,' he says. 'Others have tried, and their compounds fell. If there were less of them, we could mow them down, cart them off and burn them somewhere distant. But there are too many, and more coming all the time. So we leave them be, let them pound on the walls and circle the compound endlessly. The noise is a pain, especially when hundreds of them howl at the same time – that usually happens a few times a day, thankfully never for more than a couple of minutes – but you start to tune it out after a while.'

Vinyl turns to face the Hammersmith posse. 'I'm not trying to con you. Life is hard here, but easier than it is most places. We're experienced and wily. We haven't survived this long just by luck. We know a lot about zombies and we're constantly studying them, finding out new information, using that against them.

'We're also more liberal than in other camps. You'll be treated fairly. We share food and water equally. In some places the leaders and soldiers get more. That isn't the case in New Kirkham. We have regular meetings to decide the laws we're gonna live by. Anyone can run for office and you can be voted out at any time. We make use of people's strengths – if you're an architect, we'll ask you to work on new buildings, if you're a farmer, we'll ask you to help with the crops – but we don't force anyone to do anything.'

Rage grunts cynically. 'It sounds like Utopia.'

Vinyl nods. 'Except for the threat of the zombies, it is. I don't know if we can keep it that way forever, but at the moment it's pretty sweet. Everyone's united, working towards the same goal, for the good of the majority. In a way I'm almost glad the apocalypse happened, because I'd never have got to experience a place like this if it hadn't.'

'You make it sound enticing,' Emma says, smiling nervously.

'Come and check it out,' Vinyl says. 'If I'm lying, or if you don't like the look of the set-up, you're free to leave and we'll escort you back to Hammersmith.'

'Is that true?' Emma asks Carl, trusting him more than Vinyl, having spent the past few months in County Hall.

Carl nods. 'We're here to do whatever you want. If that means taking you back to Hammersmith or somewhere else, so be it. We won't abandon you. You have our word.'

'OK,' Emma sighs. 'I'll give it a go.'

'Excellent,' Vinyl beams. 'And the rest of you?' The humans look uneasy, but they all nod grudgingly. 'You won't regret it,' Vinyl tells them. 'This is the best decision you'll ever make.'

I wince at that – it's like he's personally inviting Lady Luck to strike us down on the spot – but Vinyl winks at me and mouths the words, 'Have faith.' And because he looks so confident and cocky, like the Vinyl of old, I find myself trusting him, the same as the others.

We check to make sure everything is in order, steel ourselves for the dangerous run to come, then head towards New Kirkham and the start of what will hopefully be a long and happy life for the humans under our care. Although if it all goes wrong, their future could end here, on the outskirts of the compound, with safety all too cruelly in their sights.

FIFTEEN

The slope leads down into a dip, then the ground rises again. When we come to the crest of the ridge, Vinyl tells us to lie flat. He inches forward on his stomach and pulls out a small mirror. He waits for the clouds to part, then starts flashing in the direction of New Kirkham, a series of short and long bursts.

'Must be Morse code,' Rage says.

'You reckon?' I jeer. 'Thanks for pointing out the obvious. The rest of us would have been scratching our heads for hours trying to figure that out.'

Rage gives me the finger. Vinyl finishes signalling

and waits for a response. When it comes, he flashes another message then wriggles back beside us. 'I've told them we're coming. They'll create a diversion.'

'Why not send a smoke signal while you're at it?' Rage asks sourly.

Vinyl chuckles. 'Don't knock the old ways. Phones don't work any more. We could use walkie-talkies, but they can be temperamental, and we'd have to lug them around everywhere, and zombies might hear the crackle.'

'Isn't there a danger they might spot the flashes and investigate?' Ashtat asks.

'It happens occasionally,' Vinyl says. 'Far less than you'd expect. Most of them can't connect the lights with human activity. They're dumb that way. Let's hope they never wise up.'

'I learnt Morse code in hospital,' Jakob says quietly, surprising us as he always does when he breaks his customary silence. 'It helped pass the time.'

'What were you in for?' Vinyl asks.

'Cancer.'

'Ouch. That sucks. Did you beat it?'

'No.'

'Does it hurt?'

Rage laughs shortly and cocks an eyebrow at me. 'Now who's asking dumb questions? Your little friend's not as smart as he thinks he is.'

Vinyl blinks. He doesn't know about the bad blood between Rage and me.

'*Any*way,' Vinyl says heavily, 'we'll be making a dash for it soon. Get ready to run. If anyone falls, the Angels will try to protect you, but obviously they won't be able to help you back to your feet, in case they scrape you.

'The rest of us need to keep moving. Don't stop or go back for a fallen friend. If you disobey that order, you'll become a liability because it means the Angels have to try and protect you too, so instead of being able to focus and do a lot for one, they'll have to split up and do less for two. Don't be a hero. That's what the Angels are here for.'

'Hear that?' Shane beams. 'He called us heroes.'

'They'll be pinning medals on us soon,' Rage sniffs.

'What about Declan?' Emma asks.

'Pass him around as you go,' Vinyl says. 'I know you probably want to take him by yourself, but it will be easier if you share the load. That way you won't get tired and lag behind.'

Emma frowns. 'Hold on. What about the tunnels you mentioned? Why aren't we sneaking in through one of those?'

'Hey, yeah,' Shane says. 'I didn't think about that. Why are we doing this the hard way?'

Vinyl shifts uncomfortably. 'Rules of New Kirkham. We don't reveal the location of the tunnels to anyone except those who are trusted members of the community.'

'You have got to be kidding,' Ashtat groans.

'Rules,' Vinyl repeats with a shrug.

'That doesn't seem fair,' Emma scowls.

'It's a safety measure,' Vinyl says. He looks around and notices us eyeing him darkly. 'Hey, don't blame me, I'm just following orders. And don't forget, I'm running the same risk as you guys. If it all goes wrong, I'm in the same boat.'

144

'It's always this way,' Pearse says.

'Yeah,' Conall backs him up. 'Don't take it personally.'

'Come on,' Vinyl says, trying to win back our confidence with a smile. 'Let's get ready to fly.'

After some dubious grumbling, we bunch up beside Vinyl and study the scene below. For a couple of minutes nothing happens. Then a group of people climb the wall inside the compound, to a large platform on the far side of town. They start hammering drums and blowing whistles. A few throw scraps over the wall.

'Brains,' Vinyl notes. 'We harvest them from our dead and keep some in stock for times like this.'

The zombies are attracted to the commotion. They race as fast as they can, or drag themselves by their fingers if they lack legs. As a mob forms, they pound on the wall, scream wordlessly for more brains, tear up the grass in search of scraps that the others might have missed.

'Does this always work?' I ask Vinyl.

'Yeah. You'd think they'd have twigged by now –

we distract them like this fairly regularly – but zombies are the dumbest creatures I've ever seen. No offence intended.'

'Plenty taken,' I growl, but jokingly.

We wait until the majority of the zombies are out of sight. Then, at a signal from Vinyl, we get to our feet and run.

Revitaliseds can run faster than humans, especially over a long distance. We could easily outpace Emma, Vinyl and the others. But that's not why we're here, so we hold ourselves in check and flank them, shepherding them towards a large steel gate that nestles in the wall directly ahead of us.

Some of the humans start to sob as we draw close to the gate. They're sure we won't make it, that they'll trip and be left behind, or that the gate won't open, or that hundreds of zombies will spring up from the earth in front of us. It's hard, daring to hope in a world where most of your hopes have been dashed and ground to dust in front of you.

We bat back a few stray zombies without slowing. One of the teenagers falls, but is back on her feet straight away. One of the men twists an ankle and goes down with a curse. The other two men hesitate, share a worried look, then return to pick him up. They scurry forward with him as fast as they can.

I scowl at Vinyl. 'So much for your instructions.'

He grunts. 'That always happens. People are too decent for their own good. I warn them out of habit more than anything else.'

Some of the zombies have started to return, figuring they're not going to get anything since they're at the back of the crowd. When they spot us, they pick up speed and lumber closer, fingers twitching, fangs glinting as they howl with hunger, alerting more of their kind.

Pretty much all of the humans are whimpering now, moaning aloud as the zombies rumble towards us, their stench thick in the air, more joining their ranks every second, a wall of undead threat.

I cast a desperate glance at the gate. It hasn't opened yet. This will be a close-run race. If the gate doesn't open in time . . .

'Do you need to signal again?' I yell at Vinyl.

He shakes his head. 'They'll open the gate when we get there,' he pants.

'You're sure?'

'They always have before.'

'What if they don't?'

He glares at me. 'Ever the pessimist.'

'I just want to know if you'd rather I kill you before some nameless zombie rips into your skull.'

'You can't fool me,' Vinyl huffs. 'You want my brain all to yourself.'

'What can I say?' I laugh, trying to fight fear with humour. 'I always had a thing for ugly, clever guys.'

The gate looms closer. So do the zombies, and there are hundreds on either side now, if not thousands, pouring towards us like two waves that are poised to meet and clash and destroy everything and anything caught between. It's not looking good. Maybe the operators inside ran into a problem with the locks and have decided it's too late to help us. I prepare myself to fight, even though I know it will be a lost cause. I see the others reach the same conclusion and get ready for the end. Rage catches my eye and snarls, 'Bloody humans!'

Then, as we're almost within touching distance of the gate, it swings open far more quickly than I assumed it could, startling almost all of us.

'I told you to trust me,' Vinyl cries out boastfully as the humans are hauled inside by the people they've travelled all this way to join. 'We have a guy who used to design theme-park rides. He was able to rig up fast-opening gates.'

'You could have warned us,' I growl.

'Didn't want to ruin the surprise.' Vinyl smirks and crosses the finishing line with his hands over his head, like a champion accepting the applause of the crowd at the end of a marathon. Flash git!

I pause in the open entrance and make sure all of the humans have made it through. Ashtat pulls up beside me.

'Don't linger,' she snaps. 'The people on the gate are alive. They wouldn't shed a tear if they had to shut out the likes of you and me.'

'Sound advice,' I grunt, then jog in with her. We're

the last two of the group. As soon as we're inside, the gate slams shut with less of a clang than I expected, blocking the way for the screeching zombies, locking us in with the residents of New Kirkham. As I stare around at them, standing well back from us, armed with guns of all shapes and sizes, looking more unwelcoming than villains in a cowboy film, I start to wonder if maybe I wouldn't have been safer on the other side of the gate with the undead.

SIXTEEN

The New Kirkhamers stare at us coldly. Some hold their guns down by their sides, but others aim openly, fingers on triggers.

'Don't worry,' Vinyl murmurs. 'They're like this every time. They don't know you, so they can't be sure that reviveds haven't sneaked in with you. Just stay calm, stand your ground and no one will get hurt.'

A stocky woman in jeans and an Aran sweater steps forward and smiles at Emma and the other survivors. 'Welcome to New Kirkham,' she booms. 'I'm Biddy

Barry, mayor of this lice-ridden hellhole. I should probably say that I hope you enjoy your stay, but let's be honest, who could enjoy a dump like this?'

As the members of the small group laugh, they're led into the heart of the compound by volunteers who chat with them softly, asking if they need anything, offering them hot food and drink. I feel happy for Emma and Declan. I can tell that they've found a good home here.

Biddy Barry faces the rest of us, standing close to the gate, huddled together as if we are the fugitives. She casts her gaze around, her smile fading, nods gruffly at Vinyl, then focuses on Pearse and Conall. 'Thanks for your help,' she grunts.

'A pleasure, as always,' Pearse says with fake sweetness. 'Now, could you ask your guys to lower their weapons?'

Biddy sighs. 'I wish we didn't have to go through this every time. I know the risks you run for us, and I appreciate it. But you're plague-carriers. If you infect just one of us, this whole place could come crashing down.'

'We're not here to infect anyone,' I snap. 'We're here to help.'

'But you can't help what you are,' Biddy says calmly. 'Accidents happen. We have to be as wary of you as we are of the monsters on the other side of that gate. Fact of life, girly. You did us a great service today, but I still don't want you edging too close.'

'There's gratitude for you,' Rage chuckles.

'You're probably a lot better than any of us,' Biddy says. 'But we're humans and you're diseased, brain-eating beasts, and that's the way it is. Now you're welcome to rest up here while the natives are settling down outside. When you're ready, we'll slip you over the wall and you can head home. I'm sure you're anxious to be on your way. Good day.'

Biddy Barry saunters off. We glance round at one another, bemused. Vinyl shrugs sheepishly. 'She's blunt but good at her job. She's been mayor for half a year, which is a political lifetime here. None of her predecessors lasted more than a couple of months.'

'She could at least have made us *feel* as if they

were thankful for what we have done,' Ashtat says quietly.

Vinyl shrugs again. 'Not many people care about the feelings of the undead. Some of the guys pointing guns at you were escorted here by Pearse and Conall, but that doesn't matter to them.'

'We're thick-skinned,' Pearse snorts.

'We don't give a monkey's,' Conall adds.

'You've got to remember that billions of people were killed by your lot,' Vinyl says. 'If you save a dozen people each . . . a hundred . . . even a thousand, that won't change what's gone down. The survivors will never forget or forgive.'

'They weren't *our* lot,' Shane gripes. 'We're revitaliseds, not reviveds. We're more like you than the zombies out there.'

'Really?' Vinyl smiles thinly. 'Do you have a heartbeat? Do you sleep? Do you breathe?'

Shane glowers at him but says nothing.

Vinyl grimaces. 'Look, I'm on your side, but I can see why others aren't and I don't hold it against them. You can't convince them that their hatred of you is misplaced because it isn't. A week without brains and you'd be hammering on the walls of New Kirkham the same as a regular zombie.'

There's a gloomy silence. This has taken the gloss off the mission. I wasn't expecting fireworks, but I did think our efforts would be greeted with at least a heartfelt thank you.

'Hey,' Vinyl says, 'don't let it drag you down. Let me show you the highlights before you leave.'

'As long as you don't expect a tip,' Rage grunts.

Vinyl laughs and leads us into the compound. Several of the men and women with guns follow closely behind, keeping watch, not lowering their weapons. It's lovely to feel wanted!

SEVENTEEN

The thing that strikes me most about New Kirkham is how clean the place is. I'd almost forgotten what towns and cities looked like in the old days. No puke stains here from feeding zombies. No blood-stains either, or corpses and bones lying in the middle of the streets. They keep it spick and span, no rubbish, no rotten food, no weeds or wild flowers.

'It's designed to be as sterile as possible,' Vinyl explains as we wind past locals who scurry out of our way, taking no chances. 'We don't want to attract insects, birds, squirrels, rats, anything that could carry the zombie gene into the compound.'

We pass some fields where they grow their own food. The farmers at work are dressed in beekeeper outfits, to protect them from flies or worms. I think it's a touch excessive, but I understand their caution.

'That's where I got this from,' Pearse says, tapping his own headgear. 'I asked them if they had any spares. This was one they were going to throw out. It has some tears and rips that make it useless for them, but it's perfect for me.'

We can see the walls again from here. Carl stops and studies them. He looks concerned. 'You might want to recommend they build the walls higher,' he says. 'I could probably jump one of them if I had a clear run.'

'And I could definitely climb it,' Shane boasts, flexing his fingers. 'My bones are like titanium. I could dig into that steel plating, no problem.'

'Angels are different to normal zombies,' Vinyl says. 'You have more powers than them. Or maybe they have similar powers, but can't realise their potential because of their inactive brains. Either way, I wouldn't mention your advanced abilities too loudly, in case the locals decide you're too dangerous for your own good.'

'We're trying to help,' Shane growls.

'They know but they fear you regardless.' Vinyl sighs. 'Anyway, the walls work with regular zombies and that's all that matters. It's not like we have to fear an attack from you lot, is it?'

'Not unless we run out of brains in London,' Rage purrs dangerously.

'Don't be greedy,' Vinyl tuts. 'We already send you the brains of people who die of natural causes. Burke told me that some other settlements do that too. You need compounds like ours. If we were all killed off, where would you get your brains from in the future?'

I spot a group of girls skipping and playing games. It seems so long ago since I was in their position. I never did much skipping on the streets, but I used to train in the local boxing gym when I was younger and I'd often test out the ropes there. I had swift feet according to my coach. Then I hit my teens and lost interest.

'How many people live here?' I ask.

'Just under a thousand, give or take,' Vinyl says.

'And how many more do you reckon the compound can hold?'

He shrugs. 'As long as we can keep ferrying in supplies from outside, we could easily treble our numbers. But if we ever got cut off from the outside world, fifteen hundred or thereabouts is probably the max.'

'What would happen if there were three thousand here and you got penned in and couldn't slip out any more?'

He grins humourlessly. 'Last in, first out.'

'Seriously?'

He nods. 'It's not like we'd throw the likes of Emma and Declan over the wall if that happened tomorrow. Chances are it would be a gradual process and we'd have time to adapt. But if the worst came to the worst, we'd let them leave through the tunnels, give them weapons and food, point them in the direction of the nearest army-run compound.'

'What if they didn't want to leave?' Ashtat asks.

Vinyl shakes his head. 'We have a good thing going. We run a civilised ship. But I'm not going to claim that it's perfect, that we wouldn't turn nasty if the situation changed and we found ourselves with our backs to the wall. This is a hard world. We can be hard too, if we need to be.'

We press on, Vinyl trying to lift the mood by telling us some more about the town's recent history, the race they faced to build the walls, how they fended off the zombies while they were working.

We're eyed bleakly by most of the people we pass. I don't mind the uneasy looks, but I'm surprised when a gang of guys treat us with actual contempt. They jeer and spit, call Ashtat crude names, and lob racist insults Vinyl's way. I bristle and turn to square up to them.

'Leave it,' Vinyl snaps.

'The hell I will. I'm not letting them get away with that.'

'If you tackle them, you'll be shot dead before you can take three steps,' he warns me.

I glance at the snipers who are shadowing us. Their faces are blank. 'Are those creeps racists too?' I sneer.

'Some of them,' Vinyl says as we move forward again. 'Not all of the prejudices of the past have been left behind. You'd think people would have enough on their plate, worrying about zombies, but old hatreds die hard.'

'Why do you let them stay?' Ashtat asks, looking angrier than I've ever seen her.

'We need them,' Vinyl says glumly. 'We can't afford to be selective. Besides, there are more of them than you might think. We've heard claims on some radio stations that the zombie virus was the result of a terrorist attack. A lot of people were wary of foreigners in the first place. This has made them even warier.'

'But you're not a foreigner,' I frown. 'You're London born and bred.'

'Yeah, but I'm a different colour to most people

here,' Vinyl says softly. 'That makes me a threat to those of a certain mindset. You should know that better than most, B.'

I stiffen, then sigh. 'Yeah, you're right. I'm just shocked that buggers like my dad are still going strong.'

'Are you kidding?' Vinyl snorts. 'This is the perfect time for them. People are never more receptive to horror stories than when they're already scared. Bigots have seized on the fears of the masses since time began and used them to their own advantage. Some things never change.'

We round a corner and Vinyl lowers his voice. 'Apparently some compounds have been segregated. Whites live separately to others, or have driven out anyone who wasn't to their liking. I've even heard wild tales that a branch of the KKK has formed in England, that its members are going round the country, imposing their order on compounds where their message of hate finds welcome ears.'

'That can't be true,' Carl says. 'The Ku Klux Klan were only in America. They never made it over here.'

'Not for want of trying, I bet,' Vinyl retorts. 'Maybe it just wasn't the right time for them before. Maybe this is what they've been waiting for.' He grimaces. 'I'm sure there's no truth to the stories, that they're being spread by idiots who want to scare people. Still, it's a sign of how volatile things are that rumours like this are circulating.

'The world crashed to its knees when the zombies ran riot. Assuming we can eliminate them, someone's going to get the chance to build civilisation anew. Zealots are already putting their plans in place, trying to ensure they get to make the world the way they want it next time round.'

Rage smirks at Vinyl. 'Sounds like it's not just the zombies you need to worry about. You might have to start whiting up.'

'Not in this life,' Vinyl says hotly. 'I'd rather die than play along with cowardly scum like them.'

'Yeah,' I say quietly, remembering that day in the school when I made my belated stand against my father. 'I know how you feel.'

'Good to have you on the team,' Vinyl smiles,

then puts the doom and gloom behind him and carries on with the tour, though it's hard for him to be as cheerful as he was after that troubling conversation.

EIGHTEEN

The racists aside, I'm impressed by New Kirkham. The people are doing their best to ignore the chaos on the other side of the walls and get on with their lives. There are schools, training programmes for adults, gym classes. Vinyl tells us there are shows most nights, plays and concerts. They've put together a well-stocked library. They have oil-run generators, but rather than rely on them, they're busy installing solar panels and they plan to construct a wind farm on a nearby hill. As well as scavenging, they make their own clothes, fashion their own spears and knives, preparing in case they ever have to shut themselves off from the world.

By the end of the tour I'm smiling thoughtfully. I have real hope for the first time that mankind can put the world back the way it was. They'll probably need us to help get rid of the zombies, but it's refreshing to see that the survivors are taking matters into their own hands, not just sitting around and waiting miserably for someone to come save them.

I'd settled into a routine in County Hall. I knew that ultimately we were supposed to be fighting for the living, but I'd forgotten what that actually meant, how much was at stake.

Now I feel re-energised. Vinyl and the others are building for a bright new future and I want to be part of that. I want to help them expand. I want to be involved.

'So what do you think?' Vinyl asks as we return to the gate.

'It's cool,' I grin.

'It needs a few tweaks,' Ashtat mutters, still angry about the racists.

'It's a dump,' Rage says. 'But as dumps go, it's OK.'

'Do you need us to send you anything when we get back?' I ask Vinyl.

'Nah,' he says. 'We're good. But thanks for the offer.'

'When will we see you again?'

He shrugs. 'Maybe when you have more survivors to deliver. Dr Oystein usually sends Pearse and Conall to fetch me. If you ask, maybe he'll send you with them.'

'I'll do that. I want to catch up more, hang out, see what you get up to here.'

'I don't know if I can promise that,' Vinyl says regretfully. 'Most of the others don't like it when you guys outstay your welcome—not that it was much of a welcome to begin with. And I can't really hop over the wall and go for a stroll with you, can I?'

Vinyl guides us to a ladder and tells us to climb up one by one. He comes last, keeping an eye on the posse with the guns, making sure nobody steps out of line. Some of them look like we've insulted them by not giving them an excuse to shoot. If there was no witness to take our side, they might be tempted to fire at us and claim it was self-defence.

It's a frightening view from the platform at the top of the ladder. We're looking out over a sea of zombies. They gibber at us wildly, unable to tell from this distance that we're the same as them, thinking we're the living come to gawp.

'Imagine waking up to that every morning,' Vinyl sniffs. 'It's even worse at night. Thousands more come when the sun goes down.'

'Have you thought about moving to an island?' I ask.

'We considered it. But most of the islands within easy reach of the coast have been taken over already, and they're very careful about who they let in. Besides, I'm not convinced they're secure. The dead don't need air, so they can walk along the bottom of the sea. They haven't figured that out yet, but I reckon it's only a matter of time. One of these days they'll realise there are juicy pickings beyond the shoreline and go in search of them. Those settlements will topple like dominoes when that happens, because they haven't counted on an underwater invasion.'

'You should warn them,' Ashtat says.

'We already tried, with the few we were able to make contact with. They laughed at us. They've grown soft. They aren't faced with a daily struggle the way we are. They thought we were scaremongering.'

There's a gloomy silence. Then Shane shakes his head. 'So how do we get down? Is there a ladder or a rope?'

'Jump,' Vinyl replies.

Shane starts to smile.

'I'm serious,' Vinyl says. 'The zombies would scale a ladder or rope. Your legs can take the impact. You're made of tough stuff.'

'But what if one of us breaks an ankle or something?' Shane protests.

'You've got the Groove Tubes, haven't you?'

'Yeah, but it's a long bloody walk back to London on a busted ankle.'

'Then my advice would be to land carefully.'

'It's OK,' Pearse laughs, clapping Shane's back. 'We're not that high up. Conall and I do this all the time. It's fun.'

To demonstrate, he steps forward, unclips a length of barbed wire, slips between two spikes and steps off into thin air. He drops silently and lands on a pack of zombies. They collapse beneath him and howl indignantly.

'Do they ever attack?' I ask Conall.

'Not if you just lie there and do nothing,' he says. 'They get irritable if you land on them like Pearse did, but they calm down when they realise you're undead. They never strike their own unless provoked.'

Conall follows Pearse's example and the rest leap off after him, one at a time, Shane under protest, muttering darkly to himself.

I wait till last, then smile at Vinyl. 'Sorry again about your mum and dad. I liked them, especially old man Vinyl and his crazy thing for records.'

'Yeah, well,' he shrugs, looking away.

'I hope it works out for you here. I'll try to come

again, but I don't know if Dr Oystein will let me.'

'I'm sure our paths will cross at some point,' he says warmly.

To my surprise my lower lip starts to tremble.

'You're not gonna cry, are you?' Vinyl growls.

'I'm a zombie,' I remind him. 'I can't. But if I was alive . . . yeah, I think I'd treat myself to some water-works. It's as good a time as any for tears.'

'You've turned into a wimp,' Vinyl smiles. 'The B Smith I knew would never have blubbed like a baby.'

'You're wrong,' I say softly, remembering all the nights I cried myself to sleep after Dad had beaten me or my mum. 'I just would have hidden my soft side and never admitted it. But I'm not bothered now. The living dead have nothing to hide.

'Look after yourself, Vinyl. Stay one step ahead of the monsters.'

'You too, B,' he sighs.

As Vinyl waves, I take a short run at the edge and launch myself from the wall, bidding farewell to New Kirkham, literally throwing myself back into the world of bloodshed, death and zombies beyond.

NINETEEN

I land in a clear spot, and though my feet sting a bit, I don't injure myself. As I stand, zombies swarm round me, growling, sniffing, opening their mouths to tear into my skull and get at my brain. Then they realise I'm like them and they withdraw, disappointed. One woman runs her fingers round the rim of the moss-encrusted hole in my chest, just to be sure.

We cut gently through the ranks of the undead, saying nothing, acting as if we're the same as any other zombie. There are some houses scattered

nearby. We'd like to seek shelter – we've been exposed to the sun a lot over the last couple of days and we're suffering, even though we're covered in thick clothes and wearing hats or hoods – but every house is packed with zombies, waiting for night to fall.

We push on, back the way we came, over the hill. A few hours into our march, we come to some trees, where we can rest in the shade. We all lie down and start removing our clothes to air our skin. I'm not sunburnt but I'm itchy as hell. I'd love to scratch but I can't, not with my fingerbones—I'd rip the flesh apart.

'This is what I hate about these missions,' Conall grunts, peeling off a pair of thermals which he was wearing beneath his trousers. 'It would be much easier if we could do them at night.'

'Yeah,' Pearse says, 'but the night world's a lot harder on the living than the day world is on us.'

'I know. I'm just saying.' Conall shuffles clear of the thermals, then fishes a backscratcher out of the rucksack he was carrying.

'Where'd you get that?' I cry.

'I never leave home without one,' he grins.

'Have you got a spare for me?'

'Nope.'

'You could have warned us, so that we could have brought our own,' I growl.

Conall shrugs. 'What am I, your keeper?'

'You'll pick up ideas as you go along,' Pearse says. 'It's all about what you learn, not what you get taught.'

'Hark at Yoda,' I grumble, looking for a twig to poke myself with.

We rest beneath the cover of the trees, discussing New Kirkham, wondering what the future holds for the people there. Rage and Shane work out, doing pull-ups on the branches, climbing the trees, racing each other, seeing who can go highest the fastest.

I lie back and listen to birdcalls. They should send a shudder down my spine, given what happened with Liz, but to my surprise I find the noises soothing. The bird wasn't to blame for what it did. I'd have to be pretty surly to hold a grudge, especially given the fact that I've caused a lot more damage in my time than that bird ever will.

As I'm relaxing, allowing myself a bitter-sweet smile, the birdsong is drowned out by the sound of engines in the near distance, big cars or trucks. We all fall silent. We're not used to such noises. They're a reminder of our past, when the roads were always alive with traffic during the day.

'Who do you think it is?' Shane asks no one in particular.

'Probably soldiers,' Carl says. 'Heading from one base to another, or to check on a compound.'

'They're making a lot of noise,' Ashtat says, concerned. 'It will draw reviveds down upon them.'

'They'll be armed to the eyeballs,' Rage says. 'I'm sure they can deal with the attacks. They wouldn't be storming around so blatantly if they couldn't.'

The noise increases then dies away suddenly. The birds start chirping again and our tension begins to fade.

Shane and Rage resume their chase and spend the next few minutes racing around after each other.

Shane scampers up the trunk of another tree and laughs at Rage as he loses his grip and falls off. 'Stick to the ground, landlubber,' he cackles.

'Get stuffed,' Rage grunts, picking himself up. 'You have an unfair advantage. With your extra-sharp bones you can dig in deeper than me.'

'They've got nothing to do with it,' Shane crows. 'It's all down to skill. I'm as agile as a . . .' He stops and squints at something in the distance. 'B,' he says hesitantly, 'that's not your dog over there, is it?'

'What are you ranting about?' I scowl, sitting up and peering round. 'I can't see anything.'

'There,' Shane says, dropping from the tree to point.

I get to my feet and put on my sunglasses. As my focus improves, I spot what Shane has seen and my forehead crinkles with confusion.

It's a sheepdog, like the one I saw in Hammersmith and the East End. It's standing in the shade of a tree a long way off. I can't tell from here if its hair is stained with blood like the dog I saw before.

'That can't be the same mutt,' Carl mutters, nudging up beside me.

'But it looks the same,' Ashtat says. 'And there are so few surviving dogs . . . What are the chances that we would spot a different sheepdog so soon after seeing one in London?'

'Maybe it *is* the dog we saw before,' I murmur. 'Maybe it caught my scent and followed us.'

'All the way out here?' Rage snorts. 'Through zombie-infested territory, so far from its lair? Why would a dog do something like that?'

I shrug. 'Maybe it likes me.'

Rage laughs. 'She thinks she's Dr Dolittle.'

'See if it will come to you,' Jakob says as I give Rage the finger. He looks a bit happier than normal, though it's always shades-of-miserable with Jakob.

I gaze at the others uncertainly. 'Should I try?'

'What are you asking us for?' Rage jeers.

'Give it a go,' Carl smiles. 'I know you said you don't like dogs, but the rest of us do. If it comes when you call, we'll take care of it. I'd love to have a pet. It could become our mascot.'

I actually like dogs. I just got nervous in Hammersmith because it seemed strange that I should run into the same dog again after so many months. I should be even more nervous now – assuming it's the same dog – but I'm not. Maybe it's the sunshine, or the fact that we completed our mission successfully, but the dog doesn't bother me any more.

I edge into the sunlight, smiling broadly, holding my hands behind my back. 'Here,' I call, clicking my tongue against the roof of my mouth—not as easy as it once was, now that I lack saliva. 'Come to B. I won't hurt you. Are you the same dog from London? Have you followed me all this way? Do you want someone to play with? Are you lonely?'

The dog barks as I advance. I stop and try to widen my smile further. I remove my glasses too, so that it can see my eyes. The dog looks behind, as if checking to make sure that nobody's sneaking up on it. It barks again, softly, the sort of questioning yap that dogs make when they think they recognise someone but aren't sure.

'Here,' I call again, taking another step towards it.

'Come to B. No need to be afraid. I won't hurt you. I'll be your friend. You can trust me, honest.'

The dog shoots off. I reach out after it, wanting to call its name, but I don't know what it is.

Rage laughs. 'So much for that.'

My smile fades. I stare after the departed dog. It's already vanished from sight into the thick under-growth surrounding the trees where it was standing. I have the uneasy feeling that I'm being watched. I'm sure it's my imagination, but it troubles me regardless. I turn slowly, replacing my prescription sunglasses, trying to pierce the shadows.

'What are you doing?' Carl asks.

'I'm not sure. I thought . . .' I shrug, not wanting to admit my unease, sure that the others would laugh and accuse me of worrying about bogeymen. Then I reach a snap decision. 'You guys wait here. I'm going after the dog.'

'Don't, B,' Jakob says. 'You'll scare it off for good.'

But I ignore him and race ahead, brushing past the trees, ploughing through the bushes, sniffing the air for the canine's musky scent.

TWENTY

I can't see the dog but I can smell it, a thick, warm, hairy smell. Then, as I draw closer, I hear it panting. I slow down, not wanting to spook the creature. I look around as I pad after it, scanning the trees for signs of life, still feeling uneasy, as if someone has been observing me. But there's nobody there.

This is silly. I should leave the dog to its own devices. It hasn't done us any harm. Jakob was right. If it spots me coming after it, the poor thing will drop a log and run for its life. If it's the same dog we saw in London, and has been trailing us all this time, it will sever connections forever and that's the last I'll see of it.

But something draws me on. I have an itch and it's not from the sun. There's something wrong about this. I can't put my finger on it, but I've got to investigate. I feel sure that there's more to the dog situation than meets the eye.

The ground angles upwards ahead of me. The area is pockmarked with hills. I don't think this is a proper forest, just some park with a lot of trees which has run wild since people stopped tending it.

I spot the dog cresting the hill. I expect it to pause, look back and catch sight of me, but instead it picks up speed and carries on, barking twice with apparent excitement.

I slow and stare at the place where the dog disappeared from view. My feeling that something is wrong has strengthened. Part of me wants to turn back and live in ignorance. Easier to hide from your fears than face up to them.

'Yeah,' I snort. 'Like I've ever done that!'

Keeping low, I jog to the brow of the hill. I can see

the end of the park from here. There's a deserted village not far beyond. A road cuts between the two. At the moment the road is blocked with a convoy of jeeps and trucks. The truck at the front is like a bulldozer, with rams attached to knock abandoned cars out of its way. They obviously use it to clear the road when they need to.

It doesn't take me long to realise we were way off the mark about this being a military operation when we heard the drone of engines a while back. Some of the people milling around the vehicles might once have been soldiers, but they aren't any more, at least not soldiers in any regular army.

They're dressed in white robes, with pointed hoods. Seems the rumours of the KKK Vinyl told us about weren't just stories after all.

It's surreal seeing them standing there, chatting and laughing, a few urinating at the side of the road. I've only ever seen Klan creeps in films and TV shows. They were like movie monsters to me, something that didn't exist in the real world, certainly not the world of twenty-first century London. It's hard to

believe they've sprung up in this country so quickly, when they've never flourished here before, and at a time when race should mean less than ever.

But there's a figure among them who's even more surreal than the menacing, faceless bigots. This guy isn't wearing a hood or a robe. He's dressed in a smart, striped suit and is walking towards the convoy, his back to me. I can see that he has white hair, and that he's also unusually tall.

I know who it is before he stops and turns to call the dog. I know by his gait and his long fingers even before I spy his pot belly and those abnormally large, almost totally white eyes with their dark pupils like two tiny black holes leading all the way to hell.

Owl Man.

The sheepdog races to its master's side and sits to attention. Owl Man bends and strokes the dog as it licks his face. He casts his gaze over the trees of the park. He shouldn't be able to see me from where he is, through all the trees and bushes, but I'm sure his gaze lingers on me for a moment, that his lips lift at the corners, that he nods imperceptibly towards me.

Or maybe I just imagine that.

What isn't in doubt is that he's real and he's here, in league with the KKK. As I stare, stunned, one of the masked men approaches Owl Man and hands him a hood. Owl Man studies it, smiling thinly, then sticks it on the dog's head. The men around him laugh.

Owl Man stands, claps his hands and barks a command. The men climb back into the jeeps and trucks. They turn on the engines and pull out, one by one, heading after the truck with the rams.

Owl Man is last to board. He climbs in the back of one of the few open jeeps. He settles the dog beside him, then bangs on the side of the jeep and points ahead. The driver nods and presses his horn. The jeep picks up speed and overtakes the other vehicles, carrying Owl Man to the head of the convoy.

As the motorcade trundles out of sight, I retrace my steps. I should be running, but I can only stumble along in a daze. I've no evidence to base it on, but I'm certain I know where the hate-mongering vultures are going.

Owl Man has been following me. The dog is his. He tracked me when I first left County Hall and went to Timothy's gallery. He was hot on my heels all the way to Hammersmith. He must have dogged our trail as we worked our way out of London, then doubled back. He had the KKK on standby. He didn't ride out here with them—he must have got in touch with them, maybe last night or early this morning, and told them to meet him here, so that he could guide them the last leg of the way.

Owl Man is leading the KKK to New Kirkham. I don't know why he's interested in me or those who are close to me, but I'm as sure as I ever was about anything that, regardless of the broader aims of his Klan buddies, he's going there to target my friend.

He's going there for Vinyl.

TWENTY
-ONE

The others are sceptical when I tell them what I've seen and what I believe.

Carl — 'You can't know that they're going to New Kirkham.'

Ashtat — 'It is probably coincidence that our paths have crossed.'

Shane — 'You might have imagined Owl Man being with them.'

Rage — 'Hell, you might have imagined the whole thing. Vinyl told you the KKK were running wild, you spot a group of people on the move, your brain puts two and two together and comes up with five.'

'Believe what you want,' I snarl. 'I'm going back. I've got to help them.'

'How?' Carl asks. 'Even if you're right, and that *was* the KKK, and they *are* going to New Kirkham, what can we do about it? They're in trucks and jeeps. We can outpace humans on foot, but we can't match the speed of a car. They'll get there before us.'

'Not necessarily,' I argue. 'They might run into roadblocks. Or they might take it easy, figuring there's no need to rush. Anyway, we have to try. Even if they get there first, we can pitch in and help the people of New Kirkham fight back.'

The Angels are unconvinced.

'Come on,' I groan. 'This is what we're here for. What's the point of escorting humans safely to the compound if we're going to leave them to the mercies of a load of racist scumbags?'

Pearse scratches the back of his neck. 'I suppose it couldn't hurt to check.'

'It would only delay us by a matter of hours,' Conall agrees.

'And if B is right . . .' Jakob murmurs.

'OK,' Rage says. 'I can see she's won you over. I must admit, I'm curious. And if it really is the KKK, and they attack, well, it will make a change to kill living people instead of zombies.'

'You're all heart,' I sneer, then pull on the rest of my clothes and hat and set off. The others aren't far behind. They grumble about me being deluded, about the sun and how much they're itching, but they follow.

We make good time. Because we don't need oxygen, we don't get tired the way humans do. We're able to maintain a constant pace. We could even talk while we're jogging, but nobody's in the mood for a conversation.

It takes maybe an hour to retrace our steps, and soon we come to the top of the hill overlooking New Kirkham, the spot where we first caught sight of the walled town earlier this morning.

The Klan convoy has made it there ahead of us. The jeeps and trucks are parked inside the compound. As I stand, looking down, I see figures in white dashing round the buildings, herding people ahead of them. There are gunshots. Someone blows a horn, over and over.

'Bloody hell,' Carl gasps, surveying the chaos.

'Believe me now?' I ask grimly.

'How did they take over so quickly?' Ashtat asks. 'Why did the people on the gates let them in?'

'We'll quiz them about that later,' I grunt. 'Right now we've got to focus on just stopping this if we can.'

Carl instinctively runs his tongue over his lips. 'How?'

I shrug. 'We get stuck in.'

'But there are dozens of them and it looks like they're packing serious hardware.'

'Doesn't matter. We're Angels. We fight. Screw the odds.'

'She's right,' Shane mutters. 'We didn't train for battle with humans, but we can take them. We have to.'

'I'm not sure what Dr Oystein would think of this,' Carl says. 'He wouldn't want us to get captured or killed. Perhaps we should observe and follow them, then report back to him, try to rescue them later with the help of the other Angels.'

'You do that,' Ashtat snorts. 'But what you are going to be observing is me kicking arse and hammering their hood-covered heads into the dirt.' I stare at Ashtat, surprised to hear her use such language. She smiles grimly. 'I was already angry about the racists inside the compound. Now I am royally pissed.'

Rage hoots. 'That's the kind of fighting talk I like! Count me in. I could never resist a good scrap.'

Carl sighs. 'I think it's a mistake, but OK, if the rest of you are game, so am I.'

'Then we're going in,' Pearse sniffs. 'Any plan other than that?'

'We don't need one,' I tell him, trying to sound more confident than I feel. 'Hit them fast. Hit them hard. And if you kill any of them, mash their brains while you're at it. We don't want those bigoted buggers coming back to life and causing even more trouble.'

I look round. 'Everybody up for this?'

They nod, Carl reluctantly.

'Then let's go show those bastards what we're made of.'

To a roar of approval, we head down the hill and make a beeline for the besieged compound.

TWENTY -TWO

The zombies are in a frenzy, howling and hammering on the wall. I know why they're so excited. They can smell fresh-spilled blood. It wafts across to us like a heavenly scent that would set my mouth watering if those glands worked. In the world of the living dead, where there's fresh blood, there's fresh brains. They know they're missing out on a feast and they want in.

The walls and gate stand as firmly as they did before. I thought the KKK might have had to batter their way in, but they were evidently admitted without a struggle. Maybe they had spies working on the inside, or else the locals let them in because they were alive and apparently seeking refuge—perhaps they hid the hoods when they pulled up outside.

'You said earlier that you could jump this baby,' I remind Carl.

'If I had a clear run at it,' he growls, nodding at the zombies packed tight around us.

'There's space further along,' Pearse says, pointing to our left. 'The wall is extra-thick there. The reviveds don't normally mass around that section, as they can tell it's their least likely point of entry.'

'Lead on, Macduff,' Carl grunts.

We push through the ranks of the screeching undead and come to the relatively deserted spot that Pearse told us about. It's not a complete zombie-free zone, but there are less here than in most areas.

'How are we going to work this?' Carl asks, eyeing the wall and measuring his angles. 'I can get up there but what then? Do I search for a rope?'

'No,' Rage says. 'The reviveds would swamp us if they saw us climbing a rope. They'd want up too.' He thinks for a moment, then cracks his knuckles and grins. 'Let's do it like they do in the circus. You do your leaping trick and clear the barbed wire out of the way. I'll give this lot a leg-up, one by one—I reckon I can throw each of them several metres into the air. You catch them as they come within range. Shane waits till last. He can climb the wall and give me a piggyback ride.'

'Sounds good,' Carl nods. 'Shane? Still think your bones are up to the task?'

Shane cocks an eyebrow at Carl, then drives the fingerbones of his right hand through the steel plate covering the wall, deep into the concrete beneath. 'Child's play,' he boasts.

Carl starts to back up. 'Form a guard of honour,' he tells us. 'Keep any stray zombies out of my way.'

He stops, studies the wall, backs up another couple of metres, then propels himself forward without a word. He runs fast, head down. A few zombies crowd around us, but we push them away.

Carl races past me in a blur. For a second I think he's going to forget to jump, that he'll run smack into the wall and knock himself out. But then he hurls himself into the air like an arrow, tucking his arms in tight by his side, legs together, head angled back. He soars high above the rest of us, then slows and hangs in the air like a bird. I expect him to grab for the spikes above him, but instead he drops and lands gracefully in the middle of us.

'Too high for you?' I ask.

Carl withers me with a look. 'That was a trial jump. Now watch me do it for real.'

He backs up, waits for a zombie to get out of his way, then races towards the wall again. This time he jumps a step earlier than before and thrusts into the air more like a bullet than an arrow. He sails way overhead, past the top of the wall. I thought he was going to have to land on the wire or spikes and endure the stabs, but Carl has a different idea. He arcs over both obstacles and lands on the platform on the inside.

'Bloody hell!' Shane gasps.

'He should have been a gymnast,' Ashtat smiles.

Nobody challenges Carl, so I guess the guards who are usually on duty have been drawn away by events

in the heart of New Kirkham. He has the wall to himself.

Carl quickly unhooks a length of barbed wire and slips between two of the spikes. He lies down and slithers forward. I think he's going to fall off, but he wraps his legs round the spikes at the last second, catching them with the backs of his knees, so he can hang with both arms free, lower than any of us anticipated.

'Never mind being a gymnast,' Rage chuckles. 'He should have been in a freak show. Right. Who's first?'

Pearse steps forward. Rage crouches and locks his hands together. Pearse puts a foot on them and the pair count to three. Pearse pushes off with his other foot and Rage jerks himself to full attention, hurling Pearse high into the air.

It works like a dream. Carl catches Pearse and lets him swing for a moment. Then Pearse pulls himself up the length of Carl's body and clambers on to the platform.

Conall is next, then Ashtat, then Jakob. As I step forward, I squint at Rage. 'Make sure you don't *mis-aim* and throw me at the barbed wire,' I growl.

'It must be a terrible thing to spend your whole life expecting the worst of people,' Rage smiles. 'Don't worry. There's no time for fun and games. I'll throw you true.'

He's good to his word and seconds later I'm on the platform with the others. As I'm steadying myself, I spot a group of zombies below. They're trying to copy us. A large guy in overalls puts his hands together and gives a leg-up to a woman in a nurse's uniform. She falls short of the top of the wall – the guy isn't as strong as Rage, and the woman lacks our sense of coordination – but seeing them try makes me pause.

'Look,' I tell Rage and Shane.

They glance round. Rage laughs when he sees the zombies try again and fail. 'Monkey see, monkey *don't*. Now let's leave them to their failures and –'

'No!' I bark as Shane steps forward to drive his fingerbones into the wall.

'What's up with you?' Rage snaps.

'They're following our example.'

'So what? That guy throws like a girl. They won't make it.'

'Not that way,' I agree. 'But when they see you two climbing the wall, they'll try that too.'

'Doesn't matter,' Shane says. 'They won't be able to drive their fingers in like I can.'

'Sure,' I sneer. 'But they *will* be able to dig them into the holes that you've left behind.'

Shane's face falls. So does Rage's. 'I never thought of that,' he mutters.

'Well, think of it now,' I tell him. 'You guys can't come up that way.'

'So what's the alternative?' he asks.

I look to the others for suggestions.

'We could make a daisy chain,' Ashtat says. 'Pearse could hang from Carl's hands, Conall could hang from Pearse's . . .'

'I'm not *that* strong,' Carl protests.

'And getting back up would be tricky,' Pearse agrees.

I wait for more ideas. When nobody proposes any, I tell Rage to throw Shane up to us. 'You'll have to sit this one out.'

'Trying to get rid of me?' Rage scowls.

'For once, no,' I say truthfully. 'We could do with a bruiser like you in here. But our hands are tied.'

'Damn it!' Rage kicks the wall in anger. Then he sighs, locks his fingers together and gives Shane a boost up. 'B,' he calls before I disappear from sight. 'Kill a few of those bastards for me.'

'I'll do my best,' I promise, then we swarm forward into the belly of New Kirkham to lock horns with the white-hooded members of the Ku Klux Klan.

TWENTY -THREE

We creep past the empty houses and along the silent streets. Most people have gathered in the large open square just inside the main gate, where the Klan crew have parked their jeeps and trucks. Some of the residents – mainly those with dark skin or foreign accents – are running from them, trying to hide. We hear their sobs and screams as they're chased by cackling Klansmen.

A black boy no more than nine or ten years old races by us. He doesn't see us since we're keeping to shadows at the side of the street.

One of the white-clad ghouls comes jogging after the boy. He's carrying a rifle. He fires off a shot which only just misses. He curses and mutters something about the gun being faulty. 'I'll just have to use my hands,' he giggles, then starts clicking his tongue and calling to the boy as if he was a dog.

I slip out of the shadows and up behind the vile hunter. My eyes are burning. My hands are bunched into fists. I've slaughtered more than a few reviveds since I revitalised, and turned a couple of people into zombies. But I've never deliberately killed a living, breathing person. I'm not sure that I can.

The boy trips and curls up into a ball. He's too scared to get up and push on. The man laughs and flexes his fingers. 'I'm gonna make this slow,' he drawls as he closes in. 'It's gonna be painful. By the end you'll wish you'd never been –'

'Hey,' I call softly.

The man turns, surprised. Before he can react, I drive my right hand through the cloth of his hood, through the flesh of his forehead, through the skull behind that, and into the soft, squishy brain beneath.

'Guess that answers that question,' I grunt as I pull my hand free and he drops into the dirt to die where he belongs.

'On your feet,' I tell the boy, who's staring at me with wide eyes. 'Go hide, and don't come out until this is over.'

'I saw you earlier,' he whispers. 'You're one of the good zombies.'

I cock an eyebrow at him. 'I don't know if I'd go that far. But yeah, I'm not here to eat your brain. Now go –'

'They caught my mum,' he interrupts. 'They put her in a cage.'

'I'll free her,' I promise. 'She'll come find you. Now go hide like I said.'

The boy nods, gets up and scampers away. I return to the shadows at the side of the street. Ashtat studies me gravely as I wipe my hand clean on my trousers.

'Something to say?' I snap, expecting a lecture.

She shakes her head, then nods. 'I hope I can find your kind of strength when it is my time to kill,' she murmurs. 'If not, will you help me?'

I stare at her uncertainly. I wasn't expecting a compliment. I look at the others and they're gawping at me too, like I'm some kind of hero.

'Look, it's simple,' I tell them. 'These guys are the enemy. He was going to kill that boy. They're monsters, even worse than the reviveds. If there was a court we could take them to, I'd suggest we round them up and drag them there alive. But we're all the law there is out here. If they surrender, fine, we'll let the people of New Kirkham bind them nice and tightly and do what they like with the creeps. Otherwise we put them down like the savage dogs they are. Don't think of them as human. They're not.'

The Angels nod hesitantly. I can tell they feel uneasy about this. But there's no time to debate it. We have to act before it's too late.

We edge forward again. I lead the way this time, the others ceding authority to me since I seem to be the most cold-blooded of us, best suited to the dirty business at hand. And I've got to admit that the execution didn't bother me. I know that it should, but he deserved death and I'm glad I was able to carry out the sentence.

We come to the corner of a building and are afforded a clear view of the main square. Several Klanners are stationed in the centre, on top of an open-backed jeep. Owl Man stands among them, stroking his dog and whispering to it as he surveys the scene with no outward display of emotion.

Others, armed to the teeth with automatic rifles, are forcing blacks, Arabs and Asians into the backs of trucks. Some of the screaming victims have been thrown into cages as if they're livestock being loaded and taken to market.

Not all of the tyrants are in robes and hoods. At least forty or fifty of those involved in the round-up are dressed in normal clothes. I recognise a few of the faces from earlier. They're people who lived in New Kirkham, who built the walls and tilled the fields and shared food and drink with those they're now herding into mobile prisons to be taken away to God knows where. They fought together against the zombies, but now they've turned on their own. This explains how the Klanners got in and why they were able to suppress any uprising so easily—they had inside help.

And the rest of the inhabitants? Most stand by neutrally, looking ashamed and uneasy. They let this happen and say nothing, maybe figuring that if they keep silent and don't pitch in, then they're not really guilty.

That's humanity for you.

Only a hundred or so look like they put up real resistance. They're standing in a pack against the wall beside the gate, under heavily armed guard. Some are wounded and bleeding. All look enraged and defiant.

And that's humanity as well. The worst and the best, in the same place at the same time, as they nearly always are.

'You won't get away with this,' a woman roars, and I find the face of Biddy Barry in the crowd by the wall. 'We'll track you down and make you pay. This is outrageous. Those people are our flesh and blood.

This is a sanctuary, not a hunting range for cowardly, bullying white boys.'

'Shut up!' one of the Klansmen roars.

'Make me,' Biddy retorts.

He draws a pistol and takes aim.

'Now, now,' Owl Man purrs. 'I don't think we need take matters that far.'

The man curses. 'Do you want some of this, freak?'

Owl Man pulls a pained expression. 'It's such a pity when people reduce an argument to a personal, vindictive level.' His lips twitch mischievously. 'Attack, Sakarias,' he says to his dog.

In a flash the sheepdog leaps from its master's side and lands on the ground. It barrels forward at a furious speed. The guy in the hood has time to scream, but only once. Then the dog is on him. It opens its jaws wide to reveal fangs far sharper than any I've seen before, and bones slide out of its claws as it jumps, like bloody Wolverine from *X-Men*.

With a jerk of its head Sakarias sinks its fangs into the man's throat and rips it open. As he collapses, the

dog leans into the spray of blood and starts gulping. Then it rips into his ribcage with its extended claws and roots among his guts. Its tail wags happily as it works on him, while Owl Man claps and croons, 'Good doggy. Good.'

'Now *that's* interesting,' I murmur.

'What the hell kind of a dog is it?' Shane asks. He looks ill with shock.

'We'll ask questions later,' I tell him. 'If there's anyone left to ask. You guys ready?' They nod shakily. 'Then my only bit of last-minute advice is—don't piss off the puppy.'

With a wicked, reckless laugh I toss my hat and glasses aside, whirl round the corner, clash my finger-bones together, scream a challenge at the world, and lead my troop of hellish Angels into battle.

To be continued . . .